SURFACE
TENSION

Praise for

THE BURN JOURNALS

★ "Engrossing from first page to last."
—*Publishers Weekly*, Starred

"The defining book of a new genre, one that gazes unflinchingly at boys on the emotional edge."
—*Booklist*

MAYBE

"Both sweet and raw, and completely real."
—*Entertainment Weekly*

"With pitch-perfect internal monologues and touchingly imperfect details, Runyon presents us with a character we feel we know from the get-go."
—*The Philadelphia Inquirer*

SURFACE TENSION

A Novel in Four Summers

Brent Runyon

ALFRED A. KNOPF
New York

THIS IS A BORZOI BOOK PUBLISHED BY ALFRED A. KNOPF

All rights reserved. Published in the United States by Alfred A. Knopf, an imprint of Random House Children's Books, a division of Random House, Inc., New York. Originally published in hardcover in the United States by Alfred A. Knopf in 2009.

Knopf, Borzoi Books, and the colophon are registered trademarks of Random House, Inc.

Visit us on the Web! www.randomhouse.com/teens

Educators and librarians, for a variety of teaching tools,
visit us at www.randomhouse.com/teachers

The Library of Congress has cataloged the hardcover edition of this work as follows:
Runyon, Brent.
Surface tension : a novel in four summers / Brent Runyon.
p.   cm.
Summary: During the summer vacations of his thirteenth through his sixteenth
year at the family's lake cottage, Luke realizes that although some things stay the same
over the years, many more change.
ISBN 978-0-375-84446-1 (trade) — ISBN 978-0-375-94446-8 (lib. bdg.) —
ISBN 978-0-375-89168-7 (e-book)
[1. Vacations—Fiction. 2. Family life—New York (State)—Fiction. 3. Change—Fiction.
4. New York (State)—Fiction.] I. Title.
PZ7.R888298Su 2009
[Fic]—dc22
2008009193

ISBN 978-0-440-24031-0 (tr. pbk.)

Printed in the United States of America
December 2010
10 9 8 7 6 5 4 3 2 1

First Trade Paperback Edition

For Lillie, Walker, and Hope

SURFACE TENSION

13

My eyes are closed, but I know exactly where we are. We just left Purity Ice Cream, the only place we can get peppermint stick in the summer. Mom didn't want to stop, but Dad wouldn't listen to her. He's addicted to the stuff.

Mom whispers, "Did we really have to stop for ice cream?" She thinks I'm still asleep.

Dad says, "Give me a break. I've been looking forward to this for the last three hundred miles."

We turn right and head north up Route 89. It's only about a half hour now, but this part always seems like the longest part of the trip. The sounds of other cars and trucks are gone. Now it's just us and the old bumpy roads.

We swerve past Cass Park and the public pool. The yacht club. The Hangar Theater.

Now we're going up the hill, and the car has to work harder. Every turn I can picture it, even with my eyes closed. I feel like I can see every single mailbox and driveway and glimpse of the lake through the trees.

Only another mile until we pass the Glenwood Pines,

where they have the best cheeseburgers and also that old bowling arcade game. I almost want to ask if we can stop, but I don't. We're too close.

The road tilts down and I can feel we're about to pass the Taughannock Falls Restaurant and State Park. The falls overlook is a cool place to go, but we can't stop there either.

The trees are thinning out and the sunlight is shining onto my eyelids. The car is going faster. Dad's pushing it. He wants to get there as bad as I do. And Mom wants to get there more than anyone. I hear the car blinker, and I can't help it anymore.

I open my eyes. The first view of the lake from high up on the hill. The smokestacks. The power station, like two fingers pointing to heaven. The way the road curves at the cornfield. The sign for fresh strawberries. The slow turn down toward the lake.

I say, "Do you know where you packed my bathing suit?"

"I think it's in the black suitcase, honey. Under the white T-shirts."

Dad turns off the book on tape because nobody is even listening to it anymore.

We're so close. The mailbox that's shaped like the house it's in front of. The place where that famous guy used to live. The old house that nobody lives in and looks like it's haunted. My parents' favorite restaurant. The chimneys on the Wirth mansion. The place where the road dips and I lose my stomach. The house that looks like a tepee. The dairy farm and the old farmhouse. My favorite sign. The mailboxes all in a row right before the bridge and the creek. The right turn onto the dirt road.

Everything looks exactly the same as when we left. All

the cottages are still here. The Bells'. The Vizquels'. The Richardsons' big cottage at the end of the lake, and our little cottage right here on the left. We park under the pine tree in front of the garage.

Here we are. We're back. It feels like it's been forever and no time at all.

I jump out of the car, take my shoes off, and sprint down to the lake. I'm not supposed to go on the Richardsons' property, so I run straight ahead to the pine tree and then turn left and run past the woodpile. The grass is cool and slick under my feet. It must have rained today. It feels like running on sponge. I'm careful not to step on any of the old rotten apples or in the hole where the tree used to be. I'm faster than I was last year, I can feel it, but when I get to the stones, I have to slow down. The stones kill my feet, but I keep running all the way into the water. I'm up to my knees. God, it's cold. I yell because it's so cold and step back out onto the dry rocks again. It's so much colder than I thought it would be.

I wait for the ache in my feet to go away and then run back to the cottage to get my bathing suit. I want to do everything all at once. Swim and skip stones and fish and go to the waterfall and cook marshmallows.

Mom and Dad are still unpacking the car. Dad says something about me having to help unpack, but I just blow right by and run into the cottage. Where did she say my bathing suit was? Under the black T-shirts in the white suitcase, or under the white T-shirts in the black suitcase? I'm pretty sure it's in the black suitcase, because we don't have a white suitcase.

I run back down to the beach, to where the good

skipping stones are. I've got a system. I look for a stone that I can hook my index finger around. One that's smooth on both sides and thin, but not too thin.

I find a good one and stand sideways. I bring my arm back and whip it sidearm at the water. I snap my wrist so it's got extra rotation on it, and it flies over the water.

The stone slaps down, arcs back up into the air, then back to the water. I get four skips, which is okay, but not great. I do another, and it goes crazy and ricochets hard off the Bells' dock. I love that sound, like hitting a baseball with a wooden bat.

I pick up a perfect stone and whip it with everything I've got, but it just splashes. I can never get the perfect ones to skip.

I skip another one that bends between the pilings on the Bells' dock.

The next one skips a few times and then stops in the water like it hit something. I say out loud, "Hit a fish," but no one is here to think that it's funny.

I sling another perfect one and it catches the air wrong, turns sideways, and knifes into the lake. Damn, I can't do this anymore. What happened?

I think I'm trying too hard or something. I look back and see Mom and Dad are standing behind me. Dad has his arms wrapped around Mom's waist. Gross.

I stop skipping stones and go to work looking for a luckystone. A luckystone is just a normal stone with a hole in it that goes all the way through. I don't know why some have holes and other ones don't, but the ones with holes are rare, which is why they're lucky.

Even more rare than a luckystone is a luckystone ring,

which is a luckystone that has a hole big enough to put your finger through it. I've never seen one of those.

My parents say this is the only place on earth that luckystone rings exist, but I don't know if that's really true. I bet I won't find one this summer.

I've got so much to do. I've only got two weeks up here, and I feel like I'm already wasting it. I've got to perfect my rock skipping and toughen up my feet by running barefoot on the beach. I've got to swim underwater for at least thirty-five feet so I can get my swimming merit badge finally.

I've got to read a book for summer reading. That's going to suck. I love reading, I just hate reading things that people want me to read. I've got to practice soccer and go to the waterfall. I've got to go fishing every day. Oh, and I've got to practice for the school TV auditions.

This year, they're going to let a student read the morning announcements on camera for the whole school to watch, and I really want to be the guy who does it. When I grow up, I'm going to be a TV reporter for a big station in New York. Either that or I'm going to race Indy cars. Or I'm also thinking about being a Sherpa and climbing Mount Everest all the time. I don't know if my feet are big enough to be a mountain climber or an Indy car driver, though. I'm only a size 9, and most of my friends are already size 10 or bigger.

But the TV auditions come first. I'm going to be like, *This is Luke reporting from Sheldrake, New York, where everything is better than where you are. If you don't believe me, just check out the Richardsons' big white house.*

That's pretty good. I'm just going to have to keep on

working on that. I could interview myself. That would be funny.

Hi, Luke, thanks for being on the show.

Thanks for having me.

So, what do you think about the state of the world and the rest of the stuff that's happening?

I pretty much think it all sucks pretty hard right about now.

Great, thanks for being on the show.

Thanks for having me.

The sun is setting, and Mom and Dad want to watch the sunset. They ask me if I want to come with them, but I say no. I don't feel like staring at the sunset for an hour while I could be doing other things.

I lie down on the green plastic couch with the cigarette burn on the cushion and turn on the rifle lamp Mom got at that yard sale last year. The base is made out of a rifle stock, which is hilarious because Mom hates guns. She wouldn't even let me have sticks shaped like guns when I was little, but she loves that rifle lamp.

The refrigerator rattles off, and it feels extra quiet in here. That refrigerator is so loud, but I only ever notice it when it goes off. It still has those alphabet magnets that used to hold up my drawings when I was little, but all the drawings are gone now. They're in some box probably. I don't think Mom throws anything like that out.

I've always liked being here, but sometimes it takes a little while to get into the groove. I go over to the bookshelf and look at the books that are there. We always have the same six books here, and I always read all of them. We've got a book about stargazing, one about the Supreme Court, a mystery novel called *Produce the Corpse*, a Choose Your Own Adventure book, a Jackie Collins book, and a book of fairy tales with pictures from Disney movies.

I love that book. I remember when Mom used to read me that book before I went to sleep. I always liked the one about the sorcerer's apprentice, and also the one about Jack and the beanstalk. I like the illustrations—the old-time Disney cartoons. They're so much better than the new ones with the weird-shaped eyes and the long noses.

I take the Disney book and sit in the chair next to the old brown phone that weighs fifteen pounds. I love this phone. It's so old-fashioned and heavy. I feel like I'm lifting weights every time I talk on it, but I don't get to talk on it that much, because it's a party line. I'd never even heard of a party line until we bought this cottage. Everyone in the neighborhood shares one telephone line, which means we share it with the Vizquels, the Bells, and the Richardsons. Sometimes I pick up the phone and someone else is already on there. Mom says if I pick up the phone and someone else is on, I shouldn't listen, but I do anyway. Nobody ever says anything interesting, though.

I can hear some kids playing outside. I want to go out there and see what they're doing, but I can't because it's the Vizquels. They have two kids, a girl and a boy. The girl is about my age, and the boy is a little younger, but I've never played with them because of what happened with Dad's grill.

When I was really young, like six or something, Dad bought one of those charcoal grills, and he used to cook out there all the time, and we would eat at our picnic table. It was really fun. I don't remember much about it, but I liked eating the hot dogs. When we left, Dad says, he put the grill in our garage, but when we came back, it was in Mr. Vizquel's yard. I don't know what happened, but Dad was really pissed. Anyway, they had a big argument about it, and that was the last time we ever spoke to them.

Mom and Dad come back from their sunset watching. I shuck the corn we got from the farm stand, and Mom and Dad boil hot dogs on the stove inside. We sit at the picnic table and look out at the lake.

The sun is down, but the light stays in the air, like it doesn't want to travel all the way to China tonight. Mom lights a candle inside a jar to help keep the bugs away, and we just sit here together looking out at the lake and watching the sky get so dark that it finally gets black.

After dinner, we all go down to the lake and look at the stars. You can see every single star in the world here. It's not like at home, where you can see maybe a couple of stars and they're all spread out all over the place.

Here all the stars are packed into the giant black space. There are thousands and thousands of them. There are stars inside constellations that I never even knew about.

I look at the stars and think about the people who thought up the constellations. That was like thousands of years ago, and they must not have had anything else to do but sit outside and look up at the night sky and make up stories.

I try and remember all the stories I know about the constellations. I can't really remember any of them. All I can remember is the names: Cassiopeia, Ursa Major, Draco, Pegasus, Scorpius.

We all walk back to the cottage together, the three of us,

right next to each other, like three ears of corn. This is my favorite place in the world.

I'm starting to toughen up my feet. I run barefoot across the lawn and over the stones. I try not to slow down at all. I dive into the lake and hold my breath. I want to see how far I can swim underwater. I kick my legs and hold the air in for as long as I can, and when everything feels like it's going to burst, I come up for air. I didn't get very far, just to the second piling on Bells' dock. That's probably only fifteen feet or so. I'm going to have to keep working on that.

Mom and Dad and I are hiking up the creek to the waterfall. The rocks are as big as bowling balls, but they also seem smaller than last year. Or maybe I'm taller. I can stand on one and then hop to the next. The creek is pretty dry right now, just enough water to keep our feet wet, not gushing like it was that one year. I hope this doesn't mean the waterfall is dry too.

I wanted to go barefoot, but Mom made me put my shoes on in case there's broken glass in the creek bed. The stones are sharp here too, because they haven't been worn down by the lake yet. The walls of the creek are all shale, which is like a really thin rock you can break in your hand, but it's sharp as a razor when you break it.

There's just a little stream of water going by, filtering into a little pool. We step closer and I hear a plop like somebody dropping a round stone into the water. I must have scared a frog.

I see him. I see his little eyes sticking out of the water.

Dad kneels down on the stones and cups both of his hands and inches them out over the water. His hands are so slow that the frog doesn't move, even though the hands are getting closer and closer to his head.

Dad brings his hands together quick and cups the water underneath the frog, but the frog is slippery and strong and dives down deep to a safe place in the muck.

"Damn."

We keep walking. A little dog on a backyard chain barks at us until we're out of sight, and the creek walls rise up around us as we walk deeper into the wild. The road noises fade out, and all I can hear is the grasshoppers buzzing in the grass and the breeze in the upper branches.

This spot is my favorite right here, this little mossy spot where the water comes down the side of the gorge and drips like a leaky faucet. I reach up and pull a piece of shale out of the wall, and a huge clump higher up falls out too.

The gorge walls grow higher around us and we're in the shade now. The walls are twenty feet high and growing with every step.

Dad is a few steps in front of me, and he stops short and investigates something on the ground. He's blocking me, but I can tell it's something cool, because Mom is walking away from it with her hand covering her face. I can't see it yet, but I can smell something horrible. Dad has his shirt pulled up over his nose like a bandit.

I walk up next to him. It's something dead, but I can't tell what it is. It's about as big as a fox, but it could be a cat. There's not any fur that I can see, only a swirling clump of maggots on the flesh where the fur should be.

The maggots move like they're one creature, but I can see them individually. Eating through the body like it's an ice cream sundae.

Mom and Dad start walking up the gorge. I'll catch up with them.

I feel like I might throw up from the maggots and the smell of rotting flesh, but it's also really awesome. I pick up a stick and poke at it, just to see what happens. The maggots don't care; they just keep on eating.

Mom yells at me to leave it alone, and I drop the stick and start walking after them up the gorge.

Once we get far enough from the smell, Mom opens up the backpack and gives us each a rectangle of Hershey's chocolate. I put it on my tongue and let it melt.

There must be a car in the gorge up ahead. I keep seeing pieces of it, rusted metal parts decaying in the middle of the creek bed, like they got washed downstream. The walls of the gorge must be fifty feet high now, but there's a road up there somewhere. I wonder how the car got down here. Nobody could have driven it. Maybe it got washed down the waterfall.

I imagine some old gangsters with tommy guns pushing it off the road and watching it slide down the gorge wall. I bet when we find the car, we'll find a dead body in the trunk with bullet holes in it.

We walk up the creek bed, through the S turns, and I see the car in the weeds off to the right. I walk over to check it out.

There are no doors or windows, and even the steering wheel is gone. The seats are just wire springs, and the trunk doesn't have bullet holes, it's just rusty. It's just a busted-up old skeleton of a car. It's not that exciting.

Mom and Dad kept walking while I was stopped looking

at the car. I hurry across the stones to catch up with them. I can just start to hear the waterfall now. I think I can hear the sound of water against stones.

We turn the corner, but we're not there yet. The water is getting louder and I can almost feel it now. I can almost feel the mist and the spray, but I know I'm just imagining it.

I can't wait to turn that next corner and see the waterfall again. My heart is jumping in my chest and I'm running across the rocks.

I get to the last turn. I know that as soon as I get past these trees on the left, I'll be able to see it.

I hop up onto a big boulder and look up at the waterfall. It's not like I remember it. There's not much water this year. In other years, the water would be rampaging down the center of the stones, but now it's just trickling.

I move across the stones, cross the stream, and get up to where the water is bouncing off one of the bigger rocks. I take off my shoes and socks and wade into the shallow water. There's still enough water to dip my head under the falling water, and it feels like a cold, heavy shower on my head.

Dad tells me to climb up the side of the waterfall so he can take my picture. I climb up and raise my arms above my head, like a gymnast after a really sweet dismount. Dad takes the picture.

Even though there's not that much water, I feel happy just being here. I look up at the gorge walls, where the shale is crumbling. Now the gorge is over a hundred feet tall, but the waterfall is always cutting through it at the top, so it's probably only forty feet. I always wonder what else is up there.

There's a few burned logs and a bunch of beer cans next

to us in the woods. Somebody must have camped here recently. I want to do that. Mom opens up the backpack and pulls out a bunch of snacks for us.

I sit down on the ledge, right before the drop-off where the pool at the base of the waterfall gets super deep, and lean back against the rock. It's not comfortable, but I'm not moving either. Under the water, my toes look bigger than they do in real life.

Mom brings me over another rectangle of chocolate and a can of soda. A bunch of minnows are swimming around my feet. One swims between my toes and nibbles. It tickles, but I don't move, and now the minnows are swarming around my toes taking little bites and then swimming away.

They're tickling my feet so much I start laughing. Mom takes pictures of me and the waterfall and my feet and the minnows. This is the best.

We're all sitting at the picnic table finishing our breakfast. Dad made pancakes, and it's just the best thing to be sitting out here and looking out at the lake, eating pancakes. Mom says, "It's so serene."

Dad says, "Serene. Serene."

I don't say anything. Mr. Richardson comes over in his Sunday church clothes and asks if we'd mind if he started mowing the lawn. Dad says it's okay, and Mr. Richardson thanks him and says, "Got my kids coming down today to help get this cottage in order. Can't have it looking so rundown." He gestures over his shoulder at the cottage, which is perfect in every way.

He goes inside, takes off his church suit, puts on his sweatpants and a T-shirt, and starts mowing his whole lawn.

He mows it every Sunday after church. He's like sixty or something. He does it the same way every time. He starts in the corner near the woodpile and mows diagonally across the lawn. He mows around the trees and under the clothesline all the way up to the edge of our property, then pushes the lawn mower all the way back to the edge of his house. It's a big lawn, and if I were him and I owned a big house like he does and my own business, I'd pay someone to mow my lawn. I don't know if he likes doing it or if he's just a cheapskate, but he does it himself every Sunday.

We finish our pancakes and bring everything back inside. Mom washes the dishes in one half of the sink while Dad rinses them and I dry them and put them away. There's only three of us, so we don't really have too many dishes and it doesn't take long. I sit at the kitchen table with my copy of *Animal Farm* and look out the side window.

Mr. Richardson gets finished with the mowing and rolls the lawn mower back into the garage. Mike, the oldest, drives in first. He drives a black pickup with a V-8 engine. He's also got a sweet-ass purple speedboat with a 200-horsepower outboard motor and a girlfriend named Eliza with blond hair, but he doesn't have them with him today.

Mrs. Richardson comes out and gives Mike a hug and then goes back inside. Mr. Richardson shakes Mike's hand like they're business partners, and Mike goes into the garage and gets out the grass collector. The lawn mower doesn't have a bag on it, so the cut grass gets spread across the lawn. Mike rolls over Mr. Richardson's diagonal lines with the grass collector and then empties the grass into a huge pile on the edge of the creek.

Joe shows up next. The middle one. He's just got a little

hatchback with nothing special about it and a girlfriend named Danielle, who's short with black hair and wears glasses. Joe's cool because he plays guitar in a band, but he's much quieter than Mike. He's usually either reading or practicing guitar, but today is a workday, so he gets the ladder out of the garage and pushes it up against the house and starts cleaning out the gutters. Our gutters have little trees growing in them.

Mary, the daughter, shows up last in her little red Volkswagen Beetle. She's got blond hair and blue eyes, but no boyfriend that I've ever seen. She gets a bucket of paint out of the garage and touches up some of the trim around the house.

They take a break for lunch and go inside, and I grab my book and go down to the beach to see if I can hear anything. They're all sitting on the screened-in porch talking and laughing. I can't see them because it's dark in there and sunny out here. Mike and Joe are making fun of Mary.

I just sit and listen to them from over on our little part of the beach. I sit in a folding lawn chair and pretend to read about the pigs.

After a while, the men come outside and I can hear the sound of metal clanging against metal. I guess they got enough work done for today, because Mike and Joe are playing horseshoes and drinking beer. I get up out of my chair and go up behind the woodpile so I can see them better.

There's two railroad spikes in little pits about forty feet apart, and Mike and Joe stand on either side of the one that's farther away from me and throw the horseshoes toward the one that I'm hiding close to. I guess you're supposed to throw the horseshoe and get it around the spike. I think you get a point for getting it close too. You must, because why else would they say "Close only counts in horseshoes and hand grenades"?

Both guys are pretty good. They hit the spike on both of their throws. They walk down toward me and count up their points. They measure the distance between the horseshoes and the spike with another horseshoe. Mike says, "These are dead," and Joe nods.

I don't know how the scoring works, but I like watching them play. They throw a few more rounds, and I get bored, so I go back to my chair and just listen to the metal bang against metal.

When the boys finish their game, the whole family except Mary goes out to the dock to swim. Mr. Richardson has so much hair on his back he looks like one of those old silverback gorillas. Mike is going bald already, but Joe still has all his hair. They both have almost the same body. Big shoulders, huge abs, and Adam's apples. I wonder if I'm ever going to have one of those. I feel my throat. I don't think I'm going to, because my dad doesn't have one.

Joe stands up on one of the dock's posts and raises his arms and one leg like the Karate Kid, then jumps off in a perfect swan dive that he folds in at the last second, disappearing under the water. He comes up thirty feet away and shakes out his hair.

Mr. Richardson has jumped in too and brought a bar of soap with him. He's going to take a bath in the lake, I guess. Now everybody is doing it. Lathering up their faces and armpits and then passing the soap to the next person. That's pretty weird. I don't know why they don't just take showers. They pull some shampoo from somewhere and take a big family bath with their swimsuits on.

After the bath, they take a boat out and water-ski. They go two at a time, first Mr. and Mrs. Richardson, with Mike driving the boat. Then Mike and Joe. They're like a water show out there. They cross the wake and go under each other's lines. They hold the handle between their knees and drop a ski whenever they want. I wonder where Mary is. I haven't seen her for a while.

I get up and head back to our cottage. I walk the property line and look over to see if I can get a glimpse of Mary. Nothing. Her car is still here, though, so she must be somewhere. I get back to the cottage and Dad is inspecting the canoe and Mom is getting some chicken ready for dinner.

I don't want to do anything with my family. I want to be out on the boat with the Richardsons. I'd give anything to be a part of their family instead of mine.

Dad and his buddies Roger and Norm are off golfing. I didn't want to go with them because I hate golf. I'd rather just hang out and swim and do whatever. I mean, that's the whole point of having this cottage in the first place, isn't it? It just seems stupid to own this little cottage that's barely even a shack compared to the Richardsons' and then spend half your time out drinking in the sun on some golf course.

My parents still have a few really good friends around here from when we lived here, and they come out and spend the day with us. We bought this place when I was six. I remember how it was driving in here for the first time. I'd fallen asleep in the back, so the drive didn't seem to take too long, and when I woke up, everything was perfect. I remember everything glowing gold in the sunlight, and walking down the hallway to my bedroom. My bed was covered with stuffed animals. I remember that. It felt like home right away.

I remember fishing and running around like crazy and

doing whatever I wanted that first summer. Of course, that was when we lived in town and it was only a half an hour's drive to get here. But then we moved because of Dad's job and sold our house in town. Dad wanted to sell this place too, but Mom wouldn't let him because she and I loved it so much.

The idea was we would spend our summers here, like the Richardsons do, and Dad would commute to work. But now we live so far away Dad can only afford to take two weeks off every summer. I wish we could live here year-round like the Vizquels. That would be awesome. Maybe when I get older, I can live here full-time.

I wonder what it's like in the winter.

The golfers' wives are here hanging out with Mom. I like to hang around when the women are here sometimes. I like to hear what they talk about when they're alone and they don't know anyone is listening. There are two of them here today: Kay and Bonnie, the wives of Roger and Norm. They're all sitting around in their bathing suits, drinking wine coolers. I'm skipping rocks, perfecting my form for the world rock-skipping championships, which don't exist.

Mom is talking about the new restaurant that's going to start up right next to O'Malley's. Kay says something about the owner being a drunk. Bonnie says she doesn't think it's a great idea to open a new restaurant right next to one of the best restaurants on the lake. Mom says she thinks O'Malley's is going downhill.

They'll just sit there and talk all day long. All three of them are elementary school teachers, so they all have that teacherly kind of voice, really clear and a little too loud so you can hear it in the back of the room. I sort of feel like I'm back in third grade, except my teacher is drunk on wine coolers and wearing a bathing suit.

Bonnie asks Kay about her new school, because I guess she doesn't like it. Kay says, "As soon as we started the ELA, all my time has been taken up with the standardized testing."

With my dad and his friends, they're always doing something when they hang out, like golf or poker or watching a football game. They would never just sit around in the sun and talk. I can't even imagine what they'd say.

I'm half listening to the women while I'm trying to get the exact right rotation on my rocks so they'll skip more times. The rotation of the stone matters as much as the speed, but the angle that the stone hits the water is really the key. It has to be somewhere between parallel and slightly tilted up.

The conversation the women are having has stopped making sense to me. Something about a church, a minister, and the Bells' cottage.

I stop skipping rocks for a second and try to hear exactly what they're saying, but Mom notices me eavesdropping and stops the conversation.

There's a long pause where no one is saying anything. Then Mom says, "Want to see if you can go find a puzzle in the cottage?"

I could do that, except all the puzzles have missing pieces, but I guess I'll do something else anyway. This is getting boring.

Kay and Roger brought their daughter, Claire, out to the lake with them. She's my age, but she acts like she's about a hundred years old. We've never really gotten along. She's just so boring. Maybe girls are just different, I don't know.

When we were kids and I would do something stupid or funny, no matter what it was—even if it was just smashing up broken old bottles in the creek or trying to kill minnows by throwing pebbles as hard as I could into the shallow water—whenever I would do something like that, she would go straight back to her house and tell on me to her parents.

Not even like running back and crying to them. She'd kind of calmly walk back to her house, so I wouldn't even know there was a problem until the parents came back and said, "Stop killing minnows" or "Stop breaking bottles."

I could never figure out why she hung around at all. She was just this mini-parent who would follow me around and wait for me to do something that crossed the line and then go tell on me. She once told on me for saying "Shut up" in her yard. And another time she told on me for crossing the street without permission. What the hell? What business was it of hers?

She always knew where the line was, but I never did. I never knew where it was or what it looked like. I just did whatever I did until I got in trouble.

She's inside the cottage. I guess I'll just go annoy her for a while.

She's lying on the green couch reading a book for school. I sit across from her in the old black leather chair, also known as the Bad Chair. It's the chair I used to have to sit in after Claire told on me, because my parents didn't believe in spanking.

"Hi, Claire."

"Hello, Luke."

"What are you reading?"

"Summer reading for school."

"You have summer reading?"

"You don't?"

"I do, but I don't actually read it."

"That's smart."

"Thanks," I say. "You want to do something?"

She looks at me sideways, like she's suspicious. "Like what?"

"I don't know. Something bad."

She laughs, but not because she thinks it's funny, because she thinks I'm stupid. "No thanks."

"Why not?"

"I'm not interested in doing something bad."

"Really? Why not?"

"What's the point?"

"The point is, you do something bad, and then you get in trouble."

"Why?"

"Um, because it's fun."

"How is it fun to get in trouble?"

"Have you ever gotten in trouble?"

"Sure."

"No you haven't. You've never gotten in trouble. Oh my God, that is hilarious."

"Whatever."

"No, seriously. Have you ever gotten in trouble?"

"I don't see the point of this conversation."

"Oh my God, you are such a goody-goody."

"Screw you."

"Oh, the goody-goody said 'Screw you.' I should go and tell your parents so you can sit over here in the Bad Chair."

She doesn't say anything. She just goes back to reading

her book and ignoring me. Whatever, I'm going to go rummage through the closets and see if I can find anything cool.

Our cottage has lots of weird stuff in it from the seventies. We have a box full of hippie music that's fun to listen to because it's so freaking bad. We have a lot of Bee Gees music, and this lame bald guy who is famous for playing a cornet, which is like a high-pitched trumpet. It's so bad.

There are only two tapes that are any good. One is *Woodstock* and has Jimi Hendrix on it, but that one broke because I played it too much. Now the only good one is the Beach Boys' *Endless Summer*. I love to listen to it because it reminds me of when I was little and I didn't have anything to worry about. That's what we always used to listen to when we were driving up here in the summer.

I also like that it's called *Endless Summer*. I just like the idea of that. I wish there were such a thing as an endless summer. Sometimes it felt like it when I was little. I wish it still felt like that.

The little Vizquel boy is watching me from his lawn. I don't know why. He's always watching me, and sometimes he tries to wave to me, but I just pretend like I don't see him and I'm doing something else. I feel kind of bad, because I can tell he doesn't really have any friends, but I don't want to be stuck playing with an eight-year-old all summer.

Why doesn't he just play with his big sister or something? I don't know what it is that he thinks he's going to do with me.

He's coming over. I didn't think I made eye contact, but maybe I did.

He's so little. Why would I want to play with a little kid like him?

He says, "Do you want to play hide-and-seek?"

I say, "Not really."

"Do you want to play freeze tag?"

"No, sorry."

"Do you want to play Time?"

"I don't know how to play that."

"I could teach you."

"Uh, that's okay. I don't really want to play Time anyway."

"Okay. I can play with you sometimes, if you want. I just have to ask my parents."

"Okay, I'll let you know if I want to play with you sometime."

He turns around and walks away. I don't want to be mean to him, but it's just, what if one of the Richardsons comes over all of a sudden and needs help with their boat? I can't be playing with a little kid when that happens.

The little kid's big sister walks out of her house and goes down toward the lake. She's my age, and she's wearing a bathing suit. She's got a body like a stick.

She walks the property line right past me. She's only about fifteen feet away, but she never looks up at me. Maybe she's mad because I wouldn't play with her brother, or maybe she doesn't even see me.

I watch her go all the way down to the beach. Her feet must be tough, because she just drops her towel, walks right into the water up to her knees, and then dives in.

Mr. Richardson is outside crawling around the property line. He hates our walnut tree. It's this old tree that is right next to our house, but some of the branches reach over the

Richardsons' yard, and they drop these nasty green walnuts onto his lawn.

Mr. Richardson has complained to my dad about it a lot over the years, but Dad says he's not going to do anything about it. I think it's kind of funny. I mean, not exactly funny, but entertaining in a weird way. Every time the wind blows, Mr. Richardson comes out of his house and walks through his yard picking up all the little twigs and small branches that fell out of the trees. Then he comes over to the property line and starts looking through the grass on his hands and knees for the little green walnuts. When he finds one, he lobs it back over onto our property like a little hand grenade.

I understand why he does it, because there's nothing like the sound of a lawn mower running over a walnut, but I also think it's kind of funny to kick one or two back over onto his property as I walk by later.

Mom and Dad went to the farmers' market and I'm going fishing in the pond up at the dairy farm. But first I have to find my fishing pole, which is why I'm standing in the garage getting pissed off because I can't find it in all this crap.

For one thing, there's hardly any light at all in here. You'd think that the easiest thing to find would be a fishing pole, because it's long and skinny, but it's actually a lot harder. There's just so much crap. I wish Mom and Dad would clean all this up.

It could be under the collection of flat inner tubes or with all the bent Wiffle ball bats. It could even be up in the loft with all the old mattresses. I think it used to lean up against the refrigerator that's been unplugged since we bought this place, either there or behind the oil tank, but not near the half-empty paint cans or with the bamboo and the sticks from when I tried to make a bow and arrow.

I climb over the spare pieces of wood and start going through the toy section of the garage, with the boccie ball set and the chemistry set. I remember when we got this chemistry set. Mom got it at a yard sale somewhere. It was so cool. You open up the case and there are all these little containers of powdery chemicals. And all you do is just mix them up in various combinations to do different things. I used to play with this all the time, trying to get things to explode, but they never did. I wonder if it was because the chemicals were old or because I didn't have any idea of what I was doing.

Here it is. It was lying flat underneath the canoe, with the paddles. I grab it and carry the tackle box in my other hand as I walk up Richardsons' Lane, past the farmhouse and the grain silo and the cow barn with the three hippie symbols painted on it. A flower, a peace sign, and a yin-yang. That place smells a lot because the cows just have to stand there with the suction cups hooked onto their nipples. I used to come up here with Mom and Dad when I was little just to hang out and watch them milk the cows. I don't know why, but it sort of smells good to me up here. It smells like cow crap, but it also smells good. An old smell, like mothballs or rain in August. Smells like being a kid.

One time, one of the guys let me drink some of the milk they make here. It came out of this big silver tank, and it still had all the cream in it, and it tasted so good. It made all the milk I'd ever tasted in my life taste like water. It was sweeter and thicker than normal milk, and a little bit sour too, like all the tastes that are supposed to be in there were still there. Then they pasteurize it and homogenize it and take all the good parts out. I'd never tasted anything like that. It made me wish we lived on a farm.

I keep going up the hill to the split-rail fence. I slip through and cut across the pasture toward the pond. This is practically the only time I wear shoes during the summer, because of all the cow pies everywhere.

The pond is just past the huge oak tree, near the old stone wall. Actually, there are two ponds. One has a ton of fish in it, and the other is covered with a thick layer of green algae.

I pick up a rock and chuck it into the green one. It ker-plunks and a hole opens up in the algae, then it closes back down again. I grab a handful of pebbles and whip them through the air. They land like buckshot, and then the holes disappear again. I could do this a hundred times and the algae would just keep on coming back. I wonder what it would be like to swim in there. Maybe the algae would close over me and I'd never be seen again. I would go swimming in the pond with the fish in it, but I think it has snapping turtles too, and I don't want to get my toes bitten off.

I have a special lure that I got at the fishing store. I take it out of its box and tie it onto the line. I cast as far as I can into the pond, and as soon as it touches the water, a fish hits it. They stock this pond with smallmouth bass, so it's probably the easiest place in the world to catch one.

I reel him in and hold him up. He's a really small small-mouth bass. He probably doesn't weigh more than a few ounces. He's gobbling up the air and his little eyes are bugging out. I look him right in the eye and say, "Hey, buddy. How's life in the fishpond?"

He doesn't say anything, but he kicks his slippery little

fish body once to try and break free. At least he's not a sunfish with those razor-sharp fins. A few of those have gotten me before.

I say, "Tell some of those big guys to come jump on my hook and I'll let you go, okay?"

He doesn't agree, but I pull the hook out of his lip and throw him back anyway.

I cast my lure again and catch another little one, about the same size as the first one. It could even be the same one, but I doubt it. I think I would recognize him.

This is kind of boring. I go over and sit under the oak tree and look out at the lake. From up here I can see almost the whole lake, or maybe just half of it, all the way down to the power station. There are these dark clouds over the power station and a flash of lightning. It's so far away, though, I can't hear anything. I can just see it, like a strobe light twenty miles away.

I stand up and cast again toward the center of the pond, where an old tree trunk is sticking out of the water. I think I heard once that the big fish like to hide in the shadows.

Crap, I think I got my lure caught in the tree. I pull on it and jiggle it, but the lure is stuck. That's my favorite lure—it cost me like nine bucks. I was going to go out and catch a huge fish in the lake with that thing.

I yank hard on the fishing rod, but it just bends like crazy. I don't want to go in the water with the snapping turtles, but I also don't want to lose my best lure.

I don't know what to do. Who cares—what have I got to lose? I take off my shoes and shirt and climb over the stone wall with the fishing line in my hand. The pond isn't deep—it only comes up to my knees—but the muck underneath the water is really gross. I wish I'd kept my shoes on. It feels like I'm stepping in a hundred years of wet leaves and decomposed fish bodies. I pull my foot out and take another step, and a bunch of bubbles come out. That smells really nasty, plus my leg is covered in black muck.

I take another step and my leg slips deeper this time. I've got to make it all the way over there to the tree stump. This isn't fun. It should be easy to find, though, because I've got the line to guide me.

The muck gushes and bubbles up some more nastiness. I'm just going to keep going, but the water is getting deeper. This isn't good. It's up to my hips now.

This reminds me of that song about the boa constrictor from elementary school. I hum the melody while I move so it's not quite as gross. I keep moving across the pond, but I really don't like the feeling of this. Something just brushed up against my leg.

I get to the tree and follow the line down under the water. I can't feel where it's caught. The line is wrapped around a branch, and then it goes down into the blackness. I can't see anything at all in the water because of all the silt and stuff I kicked up when I was walking. I squat down a little and reach down, following the line. It's tighter than a guitar string, and I can't reach the lure. It must be deeper than I thought.

I know what happened. The lure is supposed to swim like a minnow when you reel it in. It probably dove down into the muck and got hooked around a deeper branch. That sucks. I probably set it in there pretty good when I was yanking on it too. Well, what am I going to do?

I guess I could try to go underwater and see if there's any

way to untangle it. I think that's really the only way to do it. I just don't want to get bitten on the face by one of those snapping turtles, that's all.

I slide in up to my neck and follow the line with my hand. It's too far under there. Crap.

I take three big breaths and go underwater. I open my eyes, but there's nothing but brown water and millions of bits of leaves in front of my face. I close my eyes. Okay, where is it? Is that it? It sort of feels like it. It's smooth, but there's no hooks.

Something swims by my face and I reach my hand up to brush it away. I didn't get it. I put my feet down into the mud to try and push myself up and out of the water, but they sink into the mud up to my ankles. I twist my body upward so I can at least get my head above water, but my feet slip a little farther into the mud. I reach down with my hand to the log to try and push myself out of the mud. My hand brushes something slippery. What is that? Is that a piranha? It's biting me. Ow. I pull my legs out of the mud somehow and come up for air. I pull my hand out. A damn snapping turtle is hooked on to my finger, and my finger is all bloody. Shit! I shake my hand and the thing lets go.

I wrestle myself out of the pond as fast as I can, jump over the stone wall, and run over to my shoes and pull them on with my one good hand. I wrap my shirt around my finger and run home across the field and down the dirt road, past the silo and the cow barn and the farmhouse. I'm crying, but I don't want to be. It doesn't even hurt that much, but I'm scared.

I find Mom reading down by the lake, and she takes a look at me and stands right up. "What happened?"

I must look like a real mess the way I'm all covered in

leaves and crap. I don't want to sound like a baby, so I just say, "I got bit."

"By what?"

"I don't know. A turtle."

"Let me see." She leads me down to the water and washes off my hand in the lake. The blood and leaves drift off in the clear lake water.

The cut isn't that big. Just about as wide as a penny. I want to tell her the whole story, but I know how stupid it's going to sound.

I'm going to have to make up something to not make myself seem so stupid. A turtle jumped out and bit my finger. I caught a turtle with my fishing pole.

I just realized I forgot my fishing pole up at the pond and my lure is still stuck. I'll have to cut the line. That's the worst part.

I got a tetanus shot and two butterfly stitches, and the doctor gave me a lecture about how snapping turtles can actually break your finger off if they're big enough. I guess it was only a little one that got me, but it didn't feel like it was little.

I walk back up to the farm to get my fishing pole. There's a sign out front of the farmhouse I didn't see before. It says Free Kittens. I've always wanted a kitten.

I step up onto the porch and look through the screen door. There's a girl looking back at me from the kitchen table. She's a few years younger than me, and she's looking at me like I might be an ax murderer standing on her porch.

I didn't even know that there was a girl who lived here. I've never seen her before. She comes to the screen door, but she doesn't open it.

"Can I help you?"

I say, "I saw the sign about the kittens."

She nods through the screen. I can't really see her face, but she's got long black hair that's braided and swung over her shoulder, and she's wearing big, round red glasses.

She looks me over for a little while longer and then opens the screen door and lets me in. The inside of the farmhouse is dark and full of old wood, and it smells weird.

A cat runs under the couch and then another chases it. I see two more sitting at the top of the stairs and another in the kitchen eating from a cereal bowl. I think the smell is from all the cats.

She walks toward the kitchen and I follow her. I'm not sure what she's doing, but I think I'm supposed to follow her. It'll be really awkward if she's just going to the bathroom right now.

She opens a door on the other side of the kitchen and motions for me to come and look in. It looks like a closet from across the room, and it is, but it doesn't have food or a vacuum cleaner in it. The only thing in the closet is a cardboard box on a shelf, filled with kittens.

There's a mother cat too, and she looks up at me. She's lying on her side with the kittens scrambling around her, trying to get food. The mother cat looks really tired and annoyed at me for watching her nurse. I feel embarrassed, so I take a step back.

I try and count the kittens, but they're moving around too much. There are a lot of them, that's all that I can tell. There's one lying off to the side, not even really trying to get food. It's the littlest one and it's almost all black except for one little white mitten on the front paw.

His eyes are closed and there's all this junk in them that looks like cement holding them closed. I want to pick him up and give him some milk or something.

I say, "What's wrong with that one?"

The girl says, "He's the runt."

All of the runt's brothers and sisters have their eyes wide open and are climbing all over him, getting food, but the runt isn't doing anything. He's just lying there.

I say, "Is he okay?"

"He's the runt. He probably won't make it."

I almost feel like crying when she says that. She doesn't seem like she even cares about the runt at all. I want to reach into the cardboard box and pick him up and take him home with me. I want to do that so bad.

It's like she can read my mind, because she says, "You can have him if you want. They're free. You can take him in a week."

I can imagine what it would be like to take a kitten home. It would be the best. I could carry him around in my jacket pocket, and he would sleep on my lap and purr when I pet him. It would be so cute.

I thank her and say that I'll be back to get him in a week. I walk out onto the porch and look up at the branches and the wind blowing through them. I can't wait until I can bring my kitten home.

We're having dinner at the picnic table at dusk and the mosquitoes are coming out, but so are the fireflies, so it's kind of like the good and the bad of the insect world. The purple martins are swooping around, feeding off the bugs. Purple martins are the best kind of bird because they eat their weight in mosquitoes every night. That's why everyone has the purple martin birdhouses on the ends of their docks. Also, they're easy to spot because they have a forked tail and they're kind of purple-looking.

We're having chicken off our new grill and macaroni salad, which is all pretty tasty. Dad seems like he's in a good mood, because he's had two beers. I'm trying to figure out when I should ask about the kitten. Maybe when he's on his third beer.

Mom is looking out into the distance, out across the lake. She really loves this place. I think I see a way to get Mom to let me keep a kitten.

"Hey, Mom?"

"What, honey? Want some more macaroni salad?"

"No, thank you. I was just wondering if you ever wanted to bring a piece of the lake back with you. Back home, I mean."

Mom tilts her head to the side, like she can't quite guess where I'm going with this, but she's a little suspicious. "Hmmm. What do you mean?"

"Well . . ." I let the anticipation build a little. "If you really wanted to bring a piece of the lake home with you, I'm pretty sure I found a way."

"What's that?" Dad is already scowling at me. This is not going great, but I've gone too far now to turn back.

"Well, how about, from the farm, we get a kitten?"

Mom says, "No." Oh shit. That's the last thing I wanted to hear. How about a "Maybe" or an "I'll think about it"?

"Why?"

"I'm not interested in trying to transport a kitten all the way home."

"Why?"

"Do you even know how to take care of a kitten?"

"No, but I could ask Claire. She has a kitten."

"Do you even know what they eat or where they sleep?"

"No, but I'll—"

"I am not bringing a kitten into our house."

"Why?"

"Do I need to remind you?"

"What?"

"Do you remember what happened with the mice?"

I'm alone on the beach looking for a luckystone. I can't believe she said no. I don't understand why. I'll take care of the kitten. I'll be so good to it. She wouldn't even listen to me or let me talk. The mice don't have anything to do with it.

Last year, my best friend, Steve, and I went to the pet store in town and bought a pair of mice. We got a male and a female, because the plan was we were going to breed them and then sell them to our friends at school and make a profit.

Steve said he was sure he could keep them at his house, but his mom said no, and then I wound up with this little cage in my room. It started off with just two mice, but in a week the female was pregnant and had these huge lumps on her sides where the babies were growing. I still thought it was going to be cool, but then she had the babies and they were just these blind, wriggling little pink knuckles. And it smelled so bad. I didn't even want to look at them, they were so disgusting.

They got kind of cute when they were like two weeks old and they could open their eyes and their hair grew in, but when I told all my friends about them at school, nobody wanted to buy them. No one would even take one of them off my hands for free.

I had to take them back to the pet store. They said they couldn't resell them, but they took them back anyway. I think they used them as food for the snakes.

The worst part was that I didn't even know that the female had gotten pregnant again, and she had another litter of mice while we were driving back to the pet store. My room still smells like mice.

But that doesn't have anything to do with getting a kitten. It's not like I'm going to breed kittens in the house. I just really want one to hold and take care of. It would be so cute.

I have to find a luckystone. If I can find one, my luck will change and my parents will let me have that kitten.

I'm going through the garage, looking for anything that would be fun. The cottage gets boring on a Wednesday when no one else is here. There's the plastic boccie ball set, but no one is here to play with, and anyway, I think a few of the balls cracked when I was dropping them on the driveway.

There's the chemistry set, but I think all the chemicals are probably expired. What else is there to do? Cut up a golf ball and see what's inside it? No, that's boring—it's just rubber. There's the canoe, but it's so heavy there's no way I could carry it.

In the corner under the canoe there's that giant-ass inner tube that Dad bought a few years ago at a yard sale at a farm. The only problem is it's totally flat. I'm going to have to blow it up.

It's got a normal-type tire valve on it, so that shouldn't be too much of a pain, because I can use the battery-powered air pump we keep in the trunk.

It takes forever to fill this thing up, but it's worth it. It's so huge. It's way taller than I am. It's heavy too. I can't carry it. I roll it across the lawn, along the property line, but it's so uneven that I can only balance it for so long and then it takes on a wobble and goes down with a weird, rubbery echo. I have to lift it up like I'm in the World's Strongest Man competition on ESPN. I get it going with a little momentum and it goes straighter.

Once it hits the rocks, I give it an extra push and it rolls the rest of the way by itself and splashes into the water. A few pebbles stuck to it on the ride across the beach. The sound it made when it rolled across the rocks was sweet. It was like a laser battle in a space movie.

I jump into the lake and splash water all over it. This thing is black, so it gets really hot in the sun, but I keep it wet so it doesn't get too hot. I jump up and into it and flip myself around so I'm facing up with just my arms and ankles holding me in and my butt dipped into the water. My back sticks to the rubber a little. That's another reason I have to keep it wet.

It's just perfectly warm. It feels like I'm lying on the big, fat stomach of some giant. I close my eyes and just float. I look at the sun through my eyelids. It's all orange and yellow and pink and red. I can't tell if I'm seeing my blood through my eyelids or if I'm actually seeing through my eyelids. If I open my eyes for just a second and look up at the sun, I get a big yellow spot in each of my eyes, and then they split into two more and I can move them around by moving my eyes. And sometimes there are these strings and dots and clear things that float by like they're underwater. I can only look at them with my peripheral vision, though, because if I try to focus on them, then they jump around like crazy.

I feel so relaxed. Maybe I'll stay out here the rest of the day, just floating. My stomach feels calm finally. When I was home, all I did was worry about going back to school and if I had the right clothes for eighth grade and about that video audition. I forgot about that.

Also, before we came up here, on the last day of school, that whole thing with Brad and the water fountain kept running through my head. How he cut in front of me in line and then I pushed him out of the way and then he pushed me back.

I should have hit him in the face right there. I should have gotten in a fistfight right then. I don't know why I didn't. I didn't want to get expelled, I guess. But still, I would have fought him right there if he had hit me, but he didn't. Instead, he was like, "Meet me behind the gym after school and I'll kick your ass."

So then I was just stuck thinking about it. I kept thinking about how I didn't want to get hit in the face and how I didn't want to get beaten up. And everybody in the whole school heard about it and kept coming up to me and saying, "I heard you're gonna fight Brad. I heard you're gonna fight Brad."

It was stupid, and people were even coming up to my best friend, Steve, and saying stuff like "If Luke gets his ass kicked, you're not going to jump in, right?"

And he said that he wouldn't jump in. That was stupid too.

Anyway, by the time school was over, I was so scared I couldn't even think about fighting. I just went down the hallway and got on the bus and went home. Everybody thought I was a wimp, I'm sure, but I hope nobody remembers that next year. If everybody remembers it, next year is really going to suck.

That's what I like about being up here, though. I don't have to worry about all that stuff. I wish we could move here.

It's Thursday, and the Richardsons have gone to work.

Mary's here, though. I can't figure out what she's doing over there. She's just walking around inside the big cottage in a big pink bathrobe.

She's got a towel too. Maybe she's going to take a bath in the lake.

She's coming out of the house. She's walking over to me where I am at the picnic table. She's holding a towel and a bottle of shampoo.

She's walking right toward me. She's smiling. She says, "Hi, are your parents home?"

"No. They're out grocery shopping."

"Oh shoot." She turns like she's about to go back to her house, but she only turns halfway, like she's still deciding something. She says, "I couldn't . . . Could I borrow your shower real quick? Ours doesn't have hot water."

She's got these big blue eyes and they're wide open, hoping I'll say yes.

"Sure," I say.

"Oh my gosh, thank you so much. You're a sweetheart."

I take her inside and show her the bathroom. She goes right in and shuts the door behind her. I wonder why she's not taking a bath in the lake like her parents and her brothers do. I guess I should stay in here till she's done, in case she needs an extra bar of soap or something.

She starts the shower. The water pressure sucks and the walls are so thin I can hear her breathing in there.

I sit down on the couch and read *Produce the Corpse*. I'm at the part where the detective is about to figure out that the guy who's been helping him find the killer is really the killer himself. That's my favorite part.

The water turns off and I hear Mary getting ready to come out of the bathroom. I hold the book like I'm reading, but I'm just looking at the bathroom door.

Mary walks out with her bathrobe on and her hair wrapped up in a towel like a turban. She looks like a movie star.

"Thanks so much."

"Sure."

"See you later."

"Okay. See you later."

"Bye."

I watch her walk toward her big, perfect cottage. I wish she would take me with her. I wish I could be part of their family, but not have her be my sister.

I like my old bunk bed, even though it's not too comfortable. I like my *Star Wars* sheets. I like the two old posters on the wall from the previous owners. The Porsche poster is okay, but I really like the *E.T.* poster with the little kid's finger and the alien's finger almost touching.

I can't sleep, so I just lie on the top bunk with my eyes open and look up at the patterns in the knotty pine. I like being so close to the ceiling. When I was a little kid, I used to make up all sorts of stories about the swirls in the wood. I used to imagine they were galaxies and I was a god looking down on them. I used to like to think about things like that, but now thinking about that stuff seems boring.

I close my eyes and try to sleep, but the night here is so quiet it's loud. The bullfrogs out in the creek and the crickets chirping. The willow branches scraping against the roof. The creek working on the rocks. The dogs barking down the road. The owl hooting.

I wish I had a new book to read, because I'm already sick of all the books we have here. I wish there were a book about a kid in a cottage near a lake, and all he wanted was a kitten from the farm up the road, but his parents wouldn't let him have one, even though the kitten was free.

So the boy got this idea that if he found a special kind of rock, which only existed in this one place in the world, then everyone would understand how much he wanted that kitten, and they'd let him have it because the rock was so powerful and so special.

And after that, after he had the kitten and the rock, everyone would understand how powerful he was. And everyone would let him do anything he wanted, and he'd get to leave the stupid family in the small, stupid cottage and go join the other family in the big cottage. And he'd sit on a throne with the kitten on one side and the luckystone on the other and be the king of the whole lake.

Then he'd water-ski and take baths in the lake and always win at Boggle, and all the creatures, the bullfrogs and the crickets, the owls and the dogs, would all worship him and do his bidding. And Mary Richardson would be his queen.

We're at a baseball game in some town that always takes us like forty-two thousand hours to get to. I don't know why every time we go on a vacation, we have to drive around the whole time going places and looking at things, when all I really want to do is be underwater. Stupid Roger, Kay, and Claire are here too for some unknown reason. When are the parents going to get it through their heads that Claire and I are never going to be friends and they should stop making us spend time together?

The only good thing about this baseball game is the food. They've got everything. Hot dogs, candy, ice cream. I could eat this food every single day.

The only other good thing about baseball is the foul balls. I want to get a foul ball this year. I just want to get one if I can. I brought my glove and everything.

I bet I could catch it if one came my way. I played T-ball for one season when I was little. Claire was on that team too, I think, but she switched to softball because the boys were too competitive, or I gave her too much crap. I was good, though. I played second base and I could hit too, but then I tried to play the next year and they took the tee away and some coach for the other team pitched to us.

Claire still plays softball, I think, because she's wearing a baseball hat for Kiwanis softball, with her ponytail poking through the back. She's sitting right in front of me watching every pitch and talking to her dad about it. Her ponytail keeps switching back and forth in front of my face like an actual pony's tail. I'm trying to watch the game, but her ponytail is distracting. I want to dip the end of it into the ketchup for my curly fries. Roger would probably beat my ass if I did that, though.

Some guy just hit a foul ball so high that it went up over our heads and out into the parking lot. That was awesome.

There's a bunch of kids out there running after it. They're just sitting out in the parking lot waiting for foul balls. That is so cool. I want to do that.

I say, "Mom, can I go out into the parking lot and try and catch a foul ball?"

"What, honey?"

"Can I go out and try and get a foul ball?"

"No, sweetie. Watch the game."

"Can I go if Claire comes with me?" I could bring the mini-parent along for supervision. I don't care about the game. I just want to catch a foul ball.

Mom looks at me sideways and then looks over her shoulder at the pack of kids out there scrambling around cars and running free, and then she looks down at Roger and he shakes his head in such a tiny way that I could barely even see it.

"Not this year. Maybe next time, when you're a little older." She turns back and watches the game again. The guy at the plate hits another foul ball. This is a beauty. It arcs up and over everything, back into the parking lot, and right through somebody's windshield. That was so awesome. I could hear the window shatter. The pack of kids runs over, and some kid pulls the foul ball out of the wrecked car. I need to be out there.

"I'm not a baby." Mom just shakes her head. Dad stares straight ahead. This stinks.

Claire is spending the night, which sucks. I guess Kay and Roger had too much to drink at the baseball game, and they don't want to drive all the way home. They're sleeping on the foldout couch in the living room, and Claire is in my room on the bottom bunk.

I was so tired when we got home I just got in bed. I was going to brush my teeth, but Claire has been taking a shower for about twenty-five minutes. What is that about? This cottage is so small you can hear the water from every room in the house. It's really rude, I think, that she's taking such a long shower while I'm trying to go to sleep. Even worse, she's using up all the hot water, so even if I had wanted to take a shower, I wouldn't be able to.

Taking a shower in someone else's house is so rude. It's so much worse than anything I ever did to her when we were kids. Like the time we were playing in her backyard near the chestnut tree and I threw one of the spiky chestnut things in her hair, it got snagged, and they had to cut it out. This is so much worse than that.

Finally, she's done taking a shower. She puts her pajamas on and comes into the bedroom and stinks up the whole room with her cucumber and strawberry and minty-fresh smells. Disgusting, now I'm never going to get to sleep.

I like it here during the week because there aren't too many people around. The Vizquels and the Richardsons have to work, so they're really only around on the weekends. The Bells' cottage, right across from ours, is empty at the moment. I don't know what happened to them. They used to be around a lot.

Since they're not here, I go out on their dock with my fishing pole and some night crawlers and try and catch some bass. I cast my line deep into the seaweed bed, where the fish like to feed, but it just comes back with seaweed on it. I know it's not seaweed, because it's freshwater, but I don't know what else to call it. I'm not going to catch anything, so I just sit down on the dock and look around.

There's a storm coming. I can tell because the water in our cove is choppy, and it's a south wind, and every time there's a south wind, there's a storm. I overheard Mr. Richardson tell Mike that once.

There's a family renting one of the cottages farther down the lake. They must be from out of town, because they look like they're right out of an L. L. Bean catalog. The parents are wearing matching yellow fleece pullovers and khaki shorts, and they have two little kids, a boy and a girl, who are in matching green bathing suits. The mom and daughter are looking through the stones on their beach. I hope they don't find a luckystone—that would suck. The dad and son are getting their Sunfish out for a little sailing trip. I want to tell them that there's going to be a storm, because of the south wind, but I also don't want to talk to them, because then I'll have to talk to them.

I hear them talking in a different language. I don't know what language it is, but it sounds weird. Could be French. It looks like the dad is telling the boy how to put the mast together on the Sunfish.

The boy has a life jacket around his neck, but it's not tied. It's just hanging there. If he goes in the water, it'll pop right off his head. The dad isn't wearing a life jacket, even though he should be. If Mom were here, she'd give him a lecture.

They push the Sunfish into the water and hop on. They probably think that because there's a south wind, it's a good day to sail, but they're wrong, because I can already see the storm clouds over the power station.

They paddle out beyond the end of the dock and put the sail up, and as soon as they do, they fly out into the water.

The wind is so strong. I almost shout to them that a storm is coming, but I don't. They probably wouldn't understand me anyway.

The Sunfish picks up the wind even more and they shoot out across the water toward the other side of the lake. It's two miles from here to there, and on some days it looks close, but today it looks like there's a whole ocean between here and there.

They go farther and farther out toward the center of the lake, into the swells of the waves. The little Sunfish disappears behind a wave and then shoots back up again. Those are big waves. I've never seen them so big on the lake.

I look over at the mom and daughter. They're not even paying attention. Okay, this could be bad. What if they capsize their sailboat? What if they drown?

Nobody is here to save them. The Richardsons are gone, and they're the only people I know with a boat fast enough to get out there and save them.

I look out at the water, but I can't see the sailboat anymore. I scan the whole lake, but I don't see them anywhere. The sky is getting darker, and I see the rain like a gray sheet coming across the water. The power station is gone.

I hope those people know what they're doing. I look back at the mom and daughter, but they've gone inside. I guess I should just mind my own business and forget about it.

I've only got four days left to find a luckystone ring. It's not going too well. I know I'm not going to find a luckystone on our beach. Our beach is only a few feet long, and nothing good ever happens on it. The Richardsons' beach is about forty feet long and covered in stones, and I bet there's one there somewhere. I don't think there's anyone home at the Richardsons' right now, so I walk slowly across their beach, looking straight down. I open my eyes wide and look at every single stone.

I wish I had a metal detector that I could sweep over the beach, but instead of detecting metal, it would detect lucky-stones.

"What are you doing?"

I think it's Mom for a second, but I look up and it's not. It's Mary.

"Huh?"

"What are you doing?"

"Oh nothing. Sorry. I didn't realize I was on your property. I'll go back. I'm sorry."

She laughs. "No. I'm not mad. I'm just curious. What are you up to?"

"Looking for a luckystone."

"Oh, that's fun. My brothers and I used to do that when we were little. I almost never found one, though."

I smile at her, but I can't think of anything to say.

She says, "Okay then, I'll let you get back to it." She turns and starts walking back to her house. I want to say something to her to make her turn around and stay, but I can't think of what it would be that I would say.

I almost call out to her and ask if she wants to help me look, but I don't. She turns around anyway, though, like she can hear me thinking, and says, "Hey, do you want a ginger-bread man and some milk, by any chance?"

"Sure."

She motions for me to follow her, and we walk up the steps toward the screened-in porch. I can't believe I'm finally going inside their cottage. She opens the screen door and holds it open for me. The door creaks as I'm passing through it, and I already love this house. It smells like gingerbread and furniture polish.

There's dark hardwood floors and wicker furniture everywhere. Our cottage is filled with nasty carpeting, plastic chairs, worn-out jigsaw puzzles, and peppermint stick ice cream. Compared to our cottage, this place is like a museum. There are perfect little lamps on the tables and dark oil paintings on the walls. There are tiny closets, and stairs going in different directions. The wood floors are clean and shining everywhere.

I follow Mary into the kitchen, but I walk slowly so I can look at all the pictures on the walls. They're all black-and-white, and every one is of Mary and her brothers through the years. The boys are dressed in suits and have their hair flattened down with oil, and they look really uncomfortable.

Mary is always in a white dress, even when she was a baby, and she always has a ribbon in her hair. They're all smiling in the pictures, but Mary is the only one who looks like she's having fun. Even when they're older, the only one who looks happy is Mary.

She pulls a gingerbread man out of a jar and pours me a glass of milk. I'm about to take a bite out of his leg, but Mary stops me. She says, "What are you doing?"

"Nothing."

"You were going to eat his leg first?"

"Yeah, I guess."

"That's torture."

"What?"

"You've got to bite off his head first. Put him out of his misery."

I put his whole head in my mouth and snap it off at the neck. She says, "That's better."

I nod and smile and take a sip of milk to wash him down. She leans back against the counter and says, "Luckystones, huh?"

"Yeah. I can't find any."

"They're hard to find. You should take a trip out to Luckystone Point."

"Where's that?"

"You've never been? Oh, that's the only place I've ever found one. Take a canoe and head out beyond Goonie Island, through the next cove, to the point at the end of the big white house. That's Luckystone Point. Look in the shallow water right where the waves break."

"Okay. Thanks." I wonder if I should leave now. I don't know what to do.

"Follow me. I want to show you something." She doesn't have to say anything else. I follow her out the back door to the garage. Their garage isn't like ours, with the stupid overhead door. Theirs are cool old sliding wooden doors on a metal track, and they're locked up with an ancient, thick padlock.

Mary reaches down into a secret spot on the side of the garage and pulls out a key. She says, "Don't tell anyone where the key is hidden."

"I won't."

She puts the key in the lock, but it must be tricky to make it work, because it takes her a few tries to get it just right. I hear it click and she pulls the lock apart and pushes the garage door open with all her strength.

I've never seen such a clean garage before. Everything is all put away exactly where it should be. There's the famous lawn mower with the grass collector. A red metal container of gasoline right next to it. A washer and dryer. And a refrigerator just like ours, but theirs probably works and isn't covered in rust spots. A toy wagon full of leather basketballs, smooth as bowling balls. A wooden lacrosse stick that looks like it's from a museum and a few pairs of cross-country skis hung high in the rafters. A workbench with a hand-powered drill and a collection of screwdrivers in every size and shape, from biggest to smallest, all hanging on hooks from the shelf.

But the coolest thing I've ever seen is the decorations on the walls. Around the whole garage there are hundreds of luckystones strung on pieces of string. They look like the popcorn garlands we made in elementary school to decorate for Christmas.

Mary leads me to the back of the garage. She pulls a jar off the shelf and shows it to me. These must be the really special ones. She pours a few into my hands, luckystone rings in all different sizes, some as small as my pinkie and some as big as a Super Bowl ring. These are so cool.

Maybe this is how I get my luckystone ring. I look up at her perfect face and say, "Can I have one?"

She chuckles and says, "Sorry, kiddo. You've got to find your own. Otherwise it doesn't count."

Right. She's right. "Yeah, I guess I'd better keep looking." That would have been the coolest thing ever, except for the part where she called me "kiddo."

I ask Dad if we can get Grandpa's old wooden canoe in the water, and that's all I have to say, because he loves getting the canoe in the water. It's a monster, though. It's really heavy, but I think I might be able to carry it with Dad this year. Usually, Mom has to help too.

The canoe is upside-down on top of a bunch of old cinder blocks, and Dad and I roll it gently off of them and onto the garage floor. The inside of the canoe is filled with spiderwebs, cushions, life jackets, and paddles.

I grab the handle and pick up the front end. Dad takes the back. It's so heavy. It feels like there's a dead body in it. I have to walk kind of sideways to hold on to the handle and still move, and still I can only walk about fifteen feet until my arm gives out and I have to put it down.

Dad says, "Want me to get Mom?"

"No, I just need to switch arms." I walk around to the other side and lift it with my left arm, but it's still just as heavy. Maybe it's a little heavier, because I'm not as strong on that side. I only get another ten feet and I have to stop again. Dad just holds up his end and waits for me to pick mine up again.

He says, "Want me to get Mom?"

"No, I'm good." It's stupid that we have to walk along the edge of our property. Why can't we just cut through the Richardsons' lawn? They're not even home. It would be so much shorter.

Finally, we get it to the rock beach, and I stumble down to the edge of the water and drop the canoe. I only drop it about six inches, but Dad freaks out. "Don't drop it!"

The canoe is old and it doesn't float that well, because the wood has to swell up before it gets watertight. I hope we don't sink while we're out there.

Dad and I put our life jackets on and push the canoe out.

We paddle out past the Bells' dock and the Richardsons'. Past Goonie Island and past the buoys. We both whack our paddles against the side of the buoy, just so we get to hear the sound.

I look down where the water is leaking in around my toes, and a daddy longlegs runs across looking for somewhere to escape to.

The water that is leaking in runs to the back of the canoe because Dad is heavier. At least I've got that going for me.

The next cove isn't very big, and I already see the big white house at the point. There's a beacon on the end of the point to keep people from running their boats aground, but Dad and I paddle toward it anyway.

I didn't tell him why I wanted to come out here. I just told him about the spot and that it had a lot of cool fossils and stuff. He's pretty much ready to do anything if it involves using Grandpa's old canoe.

We land the canoe on the point, and the little rocks make a loud scraping sound against the old wood. I can feel Dad flinching in the back of the canoe.

We walk out along the point. It's a lot thinner than I imagined it. It's only a few feet wide at the widest spot, and then it thins as it gets toward the beacon. The waves lap against the rocks from both sides. That must be how the luckystones get washed up here.

I walk along the little ridge of rocks, looking into the water for the shape of a luckystone. I bend over and look in the water for so long that my back starts to hurt. Dad's doing it too. He must have realized what I'm looking for.

I stand up and stretch my back. I think I pulled a muscle in soccer practice, because my lower back is always hurting. I put my hands upside down on my lower back and try and massage the cramping muscles.

I don't want to look like an old guy, though, so I bend over again and look for my luckystone. I see a lot of rocks, but I'm not focusing on the right place or something. I'm seeing the skipping stones, but no luckystones, and definitely not any luckystone rings. I know they've got to be here somewhere. I know I'm going to find one. I know I'm going to find one.

"Hey, son," says Dad.

"What?" I look up and he's holding something between his fingers. It's a small, round stone. I hope it's not what I think it is. I walk toward him.

Shit. It's a luckystone. He holds it up to the light so I can see that the hole goes all the way through. Why did I bring him with me? I knew he was going to find one. Now everything is ruined. Now I'm never going to get that kitten.

He doesn't even look that impressed that he found it. He looks like it doesn't even mean anything to him.

I'm unlucky. Nothing ever goes the way I want it to.

Dad washes his luckystone off in the water, so it looks brand-new, and then he puts it in his pocket. "We'll put it in the cottage. We'll start a collection."

He's never seen the Richardsons' collection.

We're leaving tomorrow. The two weeks went so fast. I didn't even do anything. I only went to the waterfall once. I only went fishing twice. I didn't find a luckystone. I didn't get a kitten. My rock-skipping championship got kind of sidetracked by the turtle bite.

My feet got tough, and I can swim underwater to the end of the Bells' dock, but that's about it.

I don't even know what I did the rest of the time. Wasted it, I guess. I keep hoping Mary will come down to say good-bye, but I haven't seen her in a few days.

Mom's already packed up most of our stuff and given away the food we didn't eat. The day before the last day of vacation is the worst. You know it's going to end and you know you should be having fun, but all the fun has been sucked into a black hole.

It makes me feel terrible. It makes me feel like I want to leave right now.

I walk down to the lake one last time. I bend down and put my hand in the water, but I can't get too close because I'm wearing shoes. It's so much warmer than it was when we first got here. I want to go for one last swim, but my bathing suit is already in the black suitcase. The car is packed up and the water is turned off. So are the phone and the electricity. There's a thousand mothballs in the closet, even though all the sheets and blankets are in a black Hefty bag in the loft of the garage. Dad set off a bug bomb in the living room, so we can't even go into the cottage anymore.

Mom and Dad come up and stand behind me and look at the water, which is flat and smooth today. Dad hugs Mom from behind and I can tell they're both tearing up about leaving.

They love it here. I wish I could spend the whole summer here.

Mom says, "Good-bye, lake," and Dad and I say it too.

The lake is part glass and part gold where the sun catches a ripple from the wake of a boat that went past a long time ago. I wish it were raining.

We turn and walk back to the car.

14

The peppermint stick ice cream is melting in the backseat, and Mom is driving because Dad got tired and almost drove us into the back of a tractor-trailer somewhere in Pennsylvania.

Dad is like a little kid. As soon as we got close to Ithaca, he tuned the radio to the Ithaca College station because he knows the guy who runs it. Now we're on the back roads, and the farther we get from Ithaca, the worse the station comes in. He keeps trying to tune it in better by rolling the knob back and forth between his fingers. I ask why we can't get a new radio, one that has like push buttons and some real speakers, but he said we can't spend any money on a radio right now. Apparently, we have to spend all our money on Dad's new toy, his brand-new kayak strapped to our roof.

I swear, I think he loves that thing more than he loves us, because when he's not listening to the radio station that doesn't come in, he's staring at the kayak in the passenger mirror. He's tilted the mirror so that it's pointing straight up in the air, just so he can look at his kayak the whole time.

Ever since Grandpa died last winter, Dad has gotten into this whole kayaking thing. I think it's because Grandpa was into all kinds of outdoorsy things, like canoeing and hiking and stuff, and now because Grandpa is dead, Dad feels like he wants to do all those things too.

Which is fine, because at least it's better than how he was right after Grandpa died, all depressed and snapping at everyone all the time. Even on his birthday, he didn't want to have presents or a cake.

Then he got a little better when he put this picture of Grandpa next to his bed. It's not the kind of picture you normally see of a dead person, where they look all saintly and kind. This one is of Grandpa on the beach with the sun setting behind him, carrying this giant wooden canoe on his head. Dad says that it was taken only about a year ago.

And then Dad got all focused on kayaking. It was the only thing he ever wanted to do or talk about. So now we're bringing a kayak up to the lake with us, and I guarantee that's the only thing he's going to talk about.

I can't wait to get out of the car and put my feet in the water, but we're still a couple of miles away. We turn right on the country road, and I'm tapping my toes under Dad's seat.

The power station pumping pollution up into the atmosphere. The Wirth mansion rotting into the earth. The roadside strawberry stand, where the fruit is covered in pesticides.

The dairy farm—where that girl offered me a kitten—got sold, and Mom and Dad say they're turning the whole place into a winery. Do people really want wine that grows in a place where cows have been shitting for a hundred years?

At least some things are the same. At least the Go

Children Slow sign is still here. And all the mailboxes are still here.

We pull in and park in our old parking spot underneath the pine tree. Dad is just staring at his kayak in the passenger mirror, making sure none of the branches scrape against the kayak. I wonder if the Richardsons are here.

Mom unlocks the cottage and starts unloading stuff out of the car. Normally, Dad would be yelling at me to help her, but now he just wants me to help him untie his kayak so he can get it into the water.

Mom is getting mad. She's the only one who is moving anything into the house, and she keeps trying to slam the screen door behind her when she goes into the house, but it's got one of those stopper things that makes it close slowly. So when you try and close it hard, it just flutters there for a second and then it closes. It's probably pretty irritating for her.

There's some guy standing out in front of the Bells' cottage. I've never seen him before. He's a big, fat white guy dressed all in black, with long white hair and a white beard, and he's talking on a phone with a really long cord, like the one we have in our kitchen, pacing back and forth and talking really loudly. Who pulls the cord outside? Who is this guy?

Dad grabs the handle at one end of the kayak and I get the other and we lift it off the car and carry it down to the lake across the lawn. We don't wave or anything as we walk by, and the guy on the phone doesn't even look at us.

He has a really thick Southern accent, and I can't understand anything he's saying, even though he's talking so loudly it's making my ears hurt.

Dad says, "That's obnoxious," loud enough for the guy to

hear. I'm surprised, because normally Dad would wait to get inside to say something like that.

We get the kayak down to our little beach, but there's kind of a problem. Every year, we bring our lawn chairs down and leave them on the beach. But in the spot where we normally set up our white plastic chairs, there is a whole new set of red-cushioned lounge chairs. You've got to be kidding me.

Dad puts down the kayak on the rocks, turns around, and looks back at the dude on the phone. Dad isn't really an aggressive kind of guy, but he's got the same look on his face like he had the time that I called Mom a bitch, like he's ready to tear the guy's head off.

We just stand and stare at the guy. I'm trying to figure out what's going on here. Apparently, this guy is living in the Bells' cottage, because there are all sorts of bags and boxes of stuff everywhere. There are a bunch of kids' toys out on the lawn, but I don't see any kids anywhere.

He does have two dogs, though—Labrador retrievers, one chocolate, one yellow—that are chasing each other in and out of the house through the sliding glass door. They're running through our yard and the Richardsons' yard. They're pissing everywhere. The chocolate one just squatted and took a dump right in the middle of the Richardsons' lawn. Wow, that is not going to go over well with Mr. Richardson, considering that he spends almost all of his free time working on his lawn.

Mom walks down to the lake, past the guy, and we all stand together, just like we always do, on the shore of the lake. But I can't concentrate because all I can hear is the guy talking on the phone.

I try to skip a stone, but it doesn't skip, and the guy on

the phone starts laughing. I can't help but feel like he's laughing at me. This is really going to suck, especially if he's going to be tying up the party line all the time. I turn around and look at Mom and Dad. They don't look happy. Dad has his arms around Mom from behind, but they look about as pissed off as I've ever seen them.

The Richardsons just arrived. Mom's getting dinner ready, so Dad and I go over to talk to Mr. Richardson about the new neighbor. I used to think that Mr. Richardson hated us, because he almost never said hi or anything. He just mowed his lawn and did his own thing, but now Mr. Richardson seems really happy to see us.

Dad shakes his hand and says, "How are you, Mr. Richardson?" I've never heard my dad call another man "Mr." before.

"You joining up with the minister over there?"

Dad says, "What's that?"

"Our new neighbor says he's a minister of some church. Got the Bells to sign over their deed to him for tax reasons. Some kind of scam, that is, I tell you what."

"Is that right?"

"That guy is a con man. I told him to keep those dogs on a leash."

We all look at the dogs, still running around our yards, chasing and biting at each other.

I say, "One of them went to the bathroom on your lawn earlier."

Mr. Richardson looks at me like he's about to strangle someone. He's mad at the minister. He goes into his garage and gets a shovel. He says, "Where?"

I point and say, "Right there."

Mr. Richardson goes over and scoops up the dog shit with the shovel, brings it over to the minister's property, and drops it right in the middle of his lawn while he's still talking on the phone.

The minister stops talking and stares at Mr. Richardson as he turns and walks back toward us. That'll teach him.

It's raining, so Mom and Dad and I get out the old Monopoly board and set it up on the kitchen table. It's totally weird how dark it gets around here when it's raining. It's even darker than it is at night, except for not really. It's just dark.

I get the race car, Dad takes the top hat, and Mom takes the dog. She says, "It looks like Panda, my dog I had when I was a little girl."

Dad is so funny. He shoots her a look over his reading glasses and says, "Panda is a great name for a dog, dear." But he's being sarcastic, so it's funny.

I say, "Yeah, why did you name it Panda? Did it have trouble mating?"

Dad says, "What did you feed it—bamboo?"

We laugh at Mom, but it's okay, because she doesn't mind when we pick on her. She likes it better than when we pick on each other anyway. She just smiles and deals out the five-hundreds, the hundreds, and all the rest into three neat little stacks in front of her.

Dad does the real estate and Mom is the banker. I don't do anything except straighten up the Community Chest and Chance cards and put a five-hundred-dollar bill in the middle of the board. Mom eyes it but doesn't say anything. She's a stickler for the real rules, so she doesn't like that we put the money in the middle, but it makes it more fun. It's like winning the lottery if you land on Free Parking.

Before we roll to see who goes first, Mom makes the same speech she always does: "Now, I want you to promise me something, and I'm very serious about this."

"What?" We both know what she's going to say, but we also know that she's going to say it no matter what we do.

"I want you to promise me that when I beat you, you're not going to cry. Can you promise me that?"

"Yeah, whatever, Mom." She always makes that speech, and she always has, ever since I can remember. It used to make me mad when I was little. But now I just want to beat her.

We roll the dice to see who goes first. I get a two. I go last. I always have the worst luck. Dad lands on Reading Railroad. Mom lands on Oriental. I land on the stupid Chance space, and the card says to go back three spaces, so that puts me on the Income Tax space, so I already have to pay a hundred and fifty dollars before I even get to do anything.

Dad rolls an eight and buys States Avenue. He's smiling. His teeth are so crooked and yellow. I've never really noticed that before. It's gross.

Mom rolls a four and is just visiting Jail. I don't like the way she moves her dog. She taps it on every square like it's a kangaroo. A dog named Panda that hops like a kangaroo. Why doesn't she just jump ahead four spaces? It's so easy to do. I mean, there are ten squares on each side.

I roll an eight and land on stupid Electric Company, which is the biggest waste of time in the whole game, because no one ever lands on it, and then even if they do, I don't get very much money for it. I've got a feeling this game isn't going to go very well.

Mom has both Boardwalk and Park Place. Dad has all four railroads and most of the red and yellow properties, and all I have are a few random properties and not much else. It sucks. It's just like the worst feeling in the world, losing at Monopoly. Seriously, it's just like being a bum or something. Being totally broke with no money and no chance of ever getting any money. And plus, whoever is winning is just so happy with themselves. It's sickening. Totally sickening. It's like some rich asshole telling a homeless guy to get a job.

I just don't have the feeling that anything good is going to happen.

It might be possible if I were playing with my friends, but my parents are so competitive that doesn't seem very likely.

Mom has hotels on both Boardwalk and Park Place, and Dad has taken all the green properties right next to them, and he's trying desperately to build up some houses on them before Mom totally cleans his clock. I have thirty-six dollars, most of it in ones, which I got when Mom landed on my stupid Electric Company space and had to pay me four times the amount on the dice. Dad's got a monopoly on the orange properties. I've been sitting in Jail for the last two turns, partially because I don't have the money to get out, but mostly because it's too depressing to do anything other than sit in Jail.

It's not even the losing that bothers me that much. It's just how everybody turns into such an asshole when they're playing Monopoly. Especially Mom. She's so competitive. It's not even what she says—she's just acting so cocky and full of herself. She's been humming the same tune for twenty-five minutes. I don't know what it is, but it's so annoying.

"Can you stop humming?"

"Why, you don't like my singing?"

"No."

"Sorry."

My turn. I know I'm going to roll either a six, an eight, or a nine. And then I'm going to be out of this game.

Eight. Finally, some mercy. I hand all my money and properties to Dad and stand up and go out the screen door and walk out across the grass toward the lake. It's stupid, but now I feel really bad about myself, like really bad.

I just about want to go and drown myself in the lake. I walk barefoot through the wet grass, and all the little clippings get caught between my toes.

The rain here smells like metal. It smells like iron or something. I wonder if it's pollution or acid rain or what, but it smells like metal.

It's like it's raining copper pennies. I should get some of those pH strips we use on our hot tub and test the water around here. I bet it's filled with lead and acid and oil and poison. I bet this whole place is just filled with terrible stuff.

I'm either going to skip stones or go for a swim, but I don't really want to do either. I don't want to do anything, so I sit down on the beach and look over at the Richardsons weeding. They're amazing. They get like one day off a week, and they spend it on their hands and knees, digging weeds out of the rocks. If I got only one day off a week, that's not what I'd be doing with my time.

Mrs. Richardson looks up at me from her weeding and smiles. Wow, that's cool. I smile and wave back, and she motions for me to come over.

"Hello, Luke."

"Hi, Mrs. Richardson."

Mr. Richardson looks up from his weeding and says, "Cool Hand Luke." Older people like to call me that sometimes. It's from some old movie I haven't seen.

"Hi, Mr. Richardson. What are you guys working on?"

Mrs. Richardson says, "Oh, we're just working on our yard here. Trying to make it look nice for our big family picnic next weekend."

"Oh cool." That sounds awesome, actually. I wish I were in their family so I could come to their picnic. I wonder if I can get myself invited. "Can I help?"

Mrs. Richardson looks up at me with her eyebrows raised. I guess she wasn't expecting me to say that. "Well, sure, if you'd like to. You see that pile of sticks over there?" She points to a pile of sticks on the other side of the beach.

"Yeah."

"What we need to do is take all those sticks and branches and stuff and carry them all the way over here to this big pile." There's a huge mountain of sticks and stuff piled right in front of me that for some reason I never noticed before. That's got to be the tidiest mountain of sticks ever. "Would you mind doing that for us?"

"No. I'd like to do that." I actually wouldn't mind that at all. It's weird. At home I wouldn't ever volunteer to do something, but working for the Richardsons seems like more fun.

I'm not the weakest kid in my school, and I'm not the strongest either, but I can carry a pretty big bunch of sticks, no problem. I carry them all over, and it only takes me three trips. I try and stack them on the pile in a way that's sort of organized, but I'm sure Mr. Richardson is going to redo it later. He's just that kind of person.

I walk back over to the Richardsons to see if there's anything else I can do. I say, "So what are you going to do with that pile of sticks?"

Mr. Richardson says, "We'll have a bonfire at the end of the summer."

That's a lot of sticks. I say, "I wish I were going to be here to see that."

They both look at each other, just like my parents do when they want to ask each other something without speaking, and then Mrs. Richardson says, "Well, we just might have to move it up a few weeks so you can participate."

"Really?"

Mr. Richardson says, "Only if the wind is blowing in the right direction."

"Which way is that?"

"Away from the house." Oh right, that makes sense. He thinks of everything.

I walk down to what used to be our little stretch of beach and look for a perfect skipping stone. It's weird, because I skipped probably a thousand stones last year, but there are all new stones on the beach this year. It's like they're restocked in the winter like how they do with the fish.

I look for ones that fit right into my finger, like they were made just for me, but a little crooked still. The ones that are perfectly oval and flat are too perfect. They just never do much.

I want to bring a collection of these rocks back home with me so I can show my friends what they're like. We could skip them across the pond where the rope swing is. That's one of the things I hate about where we live—there are no good skipping stones anywhere. Once in a while, I can find one that's halfway decent, but it still doesn't skip like even the worst one from around here.

I like how when I get a really good skip on a flat day like today, the ripples are far apart at first and then get closer and closer together.

It turns out that Mr. Richardson is a really nice guy. I thought only Mary was the nice one, but ever since the minister moved in and I helped with the sticks, the Richardsons have been treating us like we're the world's best neighbors.

Mrs. Richardson even told Mom that we could cut through their yard now and that I could shoot hoops at the basket in the driveway whenever I wanted. She even showed me where the secret key to the garage is, but I already knew that. The best part is now we can use their dock. I think they feel sorry for us because our beach is right next to the minister's dock.

I get a running start from our picnic table. I run across our lawn, and theirs, and pick up speed when I get to the stone walkway. I make sure I step on the big, flat red stone because that one is always warm.

I hit the dock and run on my tiptoes because I don't want to get splinters. It slows me down, but I'm still going fast. The boards of the dock get wider where the dock makes a right turn. Most docks are straight, but the Richardsons' dock is shaped like the picture you draw when you're playing hangman. If it were straight, I could sprint the whole way, but I have to take the ninety-degree turn a little wide.

I pick up my speed again, past Mom and Dad, and hit the second-to-last plank like it's a diving board. I spring off it and fly through the air. I can see my reflection for a split second.

I hold a huge breath of air in my lungs, hit the water, and go deep. I swim with just kicking. I swim along the bottom, near the brown rocks and the clumps of minnows. I lose my momentum from the dive and switch to the breaststroke.

When my lungs are about to explode, I come up for air and turn back to look at the dock again. Mom is standing up with a worried look on her face. She's always worried that I'm going to drown. I swim back and dry off and lie on a beach towel in the sun. I close my eyes.

At the end of Richardsons' dock, we can barely even hear the minister talking on the phone. It's almost like he's not there.

We're all sitting out in the sun. Dad's drinking a beer, Mom's got a wine cooler, and I'm having a Coke. I don't get to have a Coke that often, so it's kind of a special thing. I've been ripping through this bag of Chex Mix too.

I can hear a boat motor gunning it from not too far away. It sounds like a pretty big engine, like maybe a 200 or a 250.

It comes around the point and shoots by us. It's going so fast it's almost skipping across the water, like a perfect skipping stone. It looks like there's a dude and a chick in the boat. The chick is driving and her blond hair is whipping around her face.

I think that's Mike and Eliza. They slow down and bring the boat around so it's coming right toward the dock. It is Mike and Eliza. They're down for the weekend. I guess Mike's finally got his speedboat in the water. He calls it the *Purple People Eater*, because it's made out of this sparkly purple fiberglass.

Eliza cuts the engine and turns the boat just right so that it eases up to the side of the dock. Dad and I stand up and Mike throws us a rope. I'm about to catch it, but Dad reaches in front of me and snags it. He was throwing it to me. Mike pushes a couple of those rubber protector things over the side so the sweet purple fiberglass doesn't get scratched up by the dock.

Dad sits down and uses his feet to keep the boat out away from the dock anyway. I do the same, but my legs aren't quite long enough to steady it.

Mike doesn't have a shirt on, and Eliza is wearing a bikini top and a pair of shorts. Wow, what a set of tits. She's sipping on some kind of alcoholic beverage, and she's wearing a pair of dark sunglasses. She says, "Any of you hotties want a ride?"

I say, "I do," before she even finishes the question and before I look up at Mom and get the head nod. Mike gives me a hand and I climb right into the back.

Mike says, "You guys sure you don't want to come?" I really hope they don't say they want to come. That would suck.

My parents shake their heads, push us off, and throw the ropes back into the boat. This is the best thing that's ever happened to me.

Mom yells out something about a life jacket as Mike starts the engine up again. Eliza brings me over an old orange life jacket that slips over the head, instead of the cool blue kind with the zipper. Mike and Eliza aren't wearing life jackets.

She says, "Will this fit?"

"Yeah, I think."

She leans over a little bit closer and whispers, "You only have to wear it until we're out of sight." I've got a boner.

The air smells like the perfect mix of gasoline, oil, and lake water.

The seats are white leather with purple on the sides. There are only four seats, so I sit in the back, next to the engine.

Mike guns it and the bow goes way up in the air. I have to hold on so I don't fall out into the water. My hair is blowing in the wind like crazy, and I have to squint to see.

This boat is so cool and so fast. It's like a purple bullet going through the water. I bet it's the fastest boat on the lake.

We head toward the power station on the other side of the lake. I've never seen this side up close before. Mom and Dad and I tried to canoe across once, but we got so tired of paddling we had to turn around before we got halfway.

Mike pulls back on the throttle and we slow way down. They look back and they're both laughing at me. I must look funny. My hair is blown way back and my eyes are watering.

Mike says, "Want to drive?"

I say, "Sure," take off my life jacket, and move into the driver's seat. Mike shows me the throttle and the steering wheel and says, "Have fun," and then goes over to Eliza and lights a cigarette. I didn't know they smoked.

Apparently, they don't smoke that much, because they only have one cigarette, which they pass between each other. Is that weed?

I point the nose of the boat toward the power station and push the throttle forward a little. The boat feels like it wants to go faster, so I push it a little bit more. Mike opens a beer, drinks it fast, and then crumples up the can and drops it in a paper bag with about ten other empties. Did he drink those all today?

He taps me on the shoulder and takes the wheel again. I stand in the space between them and hold on to the backs of their seats. When the boat hits a wave, my knuckles touch their sticky backs.

Mike has slowed down the boat a little so he can talk. He says, "You know the Boy Scout camp over there?" pointing back at our side of the lake.

I don't, but I say, "Yeah."

"Me and Eliza were over there one time. I was fishing."

Eliza takes over the story. "I was sunbathing on the front of the boat, you know, topless."

"Yeah." I can imagine.

He says, "And we kind of drifted over into the area where the Boy Scouts were doing their canoe races."

She says, "And I was like, 'Shit. Mike. Start the boat.'"

He says, "But the engine wouldn't start, and we kept drifting closer and closer to the canoes. I was . . ." He mocks himself trying to start the boat. "And she was . . ." He pretends he's Eliza sitting up on the front of the boat waving to the Boy Scouts.

I thought she would have at least tried to cover up, but I guess not. She says, "Oh well, they were going to have to see a pair of tits sometime."

Mike's laughing. "Yeah, I bet they didn't think they'd get that merit badge at Boy Scout camp."

He laughs harder and Eliza hits him and then they kiss. Shit, why did I quit going to Boy Scouts?

Mike guns the engine again and turns the boat back toward the dock. I guess our little joyride is over.

The road on our left and all the houses look a little different from out here on the water. There's a big house built on the edge of the rock wall that I've never seen before, with a long wooden staircase down to a fancy boathouse and a weeping willow growing next to it. The branches drip all the way down to the water.

I'm so lucky that we moved into a cottage where the land is flat and we can walk right down to the lake. What if we moved into one of these other houses and had different neighbors? That would be terrible. Even if our cottage is small and a piece of crap, at least we live next to the Richardsons.

The night feels warm tonight and I want to be outside. Mom and Dad usually go down to the lake one last time to look at the water and the stars, and I don't usually go down with them. Usually, I stay inside and read, but tonight I want to go. We walk down to our little patch of beach and get our chairs out from where the minister put them next to the woodpile. This could be nice, but now we're all aggravated because of the chairs and because of the floodlight at the end of the minister's dock.

I don't know why he put that in. I don't know what he thinks he needs to see out there. Now our whole beach is lit up like a prison after an escape.

Even Mom is mad about it. She says, "That minister is pretty sinister."

That's her idea of a joke, and Dad laughs at it.

Mom says, "*The Sinister Minister*—it sounds like a mystery novel."

She should know. She's always reading some mystery

with dumb-ass titles like *A Is for Accidental Homicide* and *B Is for Bathwater Drowning*.

I say, "I should just go unscrew that lightbulb."

Dad says, "That's not a bad idea. Let's do it."

Mom says, "Please don't. That's trespassing."

Dad says, "It'll be fine."

I say, "It'll be fine."

Mom says, "Fine, but if you get arrested, don't expect me to bail you out." Dad and I sneak out onto the dock. I've got the *Mission: Impossible* theme in my head. This is fun. I hum a little of it out loud and Dad turns and smiles at me. Now we're both humming it.

We get to the end and I stretch up, but it's a little higher than I can reach.

Dad and I are almost the same height, so he can't reach it either. But he weighs a ton more than me. He whispers, "Get on my shoulders."

He squats down and I put my legs over his shoulders. He's strong enough to lift me, and I go right up to the light.

I lick my fingers so I don't get burned and then twist it really fast until my spit evaporates. It takes a few licks and a few twists, but finally the light goes out.

I whisper, "Should I take it out?"

He says, "No, just leave it unscrewed."

"Okay." He puts me down and we run back to where Mom is sitting on the beach.

Dad says, "Good job, son."

Mom says, "You are a bad influence."

The Richardsons invite us over for ice cream after dinner, and we tell the story about how we unscrewed the lightbulb on the minister's dock. Mr. Richardson tips his head back and laughs into the night.

He seemed so stern before we got to know him. When he's just hanging out having an ice cream, he's really cool.

Mrs. Richardson is smiling and asking if we want any more ice cream. But she's not just like a grandma-type person. She's also really tough. I've seen her climb out onto the bow of their boat and balance out there. I've seen her carrying around picnic tables and canoes. She's tough.

Dad and Mom are sitting on an old-fashioned couch on the screened-in porch, and I'm sitting on this wicker chair with cushions. It's so nice here. I wish our house were this nice.

Mr. Richardson is telling some long story about something. I stopped listening a while ago. He can really talk.

Mrs. Richardson comes back out of the kitchen and interrupts him. "Bill, Freddy is here."

"What?"

"Freddy is outside."

"Oh, okay. Cool Hand Luke, want to help me with Freddy?"

"Who is Freddy?" I ask.

"Freddy the Freeloader."

I follow Mr. Richardson through the kitchen. He picks up an old margarine tub filled with food scraps from dinner. Some half-eaten ears of corn and some apple skins. I feel sorry for Freddy.

We go out into the night and stand outside. I don't see anyone. I wonder if he's hiding somewhere. I try and look into the shadows near the garage, but I don't see anyone. This is weird.

Mr. Richardson whispers, "You see him?"

I whisper, "No."

"Up in the tree."

Now I'm a little scared. I look up into the branches. There's nobody up there, not that I can see. Mr. Richardson sees me looking up and says, "Not up there. There."

He points to the crotch of the tree, where the branches split off. I see a pair of eyes looking back at me, but that's not a guy. That's a raccoon.

"You see him now?"

"No, all I see is a raccoon."

Mr. Richardson laughs really loudly. "Well, I'd be worried about you if you saw anything else."

He throws a corncob out into the lawn, and just like that, Freddy climbs down the tree, picks it off the grass, and goes right back up to his perch. He eats it with two hands, rotating it all the time to get every little piece of corn off, but the freaky thing is he's staring at me while he's eating. He just keeps staring at me.

I say, "He's a fatty."

Mr. Richardson laughs. He dumps the rest of the food on the lawn and calls out in a big voice, "This is all for you, Freddy."

When we head home, I see the minister is sitting at the end of the dock in the dark with his back to the water. I can't see his eyes, but I can feel him staring at us.

I get into bed and turn off my light. I don't feel like reading tonight. I close my eyes and I see Freddy the Freeloader sitting up in that tree staring back at me. I just know I'm going to have a bad dream tonight.

Plus, the minister's dogs are howling at some other dogs across the creek. It used to be so quiet that I could hear everything, and sometimes I would even wish I could hear a car or two just so I could go to sleep. But now the dogs are out there, and so are the raccoons, and the minister, sitting there in the dark watching us.

Roger, Kay, and Claire are here. Good God, why do we have to keep entertaining them? They're like the most boring people in the whole world. Claire annoys me just by being taller than me, plus her hair isn't even a color. It's so blond it's practically clear.

The adults head off to the beach to drink and to tan themselves. Claire prefers to stay inside, out of the sun. Maybe that's why her hair is so clear and her skin is so pasty.

She's dealt herself a game of solitaire on the kitchen table. I wonder if I can get her to talk to me.

"Hi, Claire!" I pretend that I'm really excited to see her, just to see if I can get her to react.

"Hello, Luke."

"What are you up to, you old badass, you?" She hates when I swear. She almost looks up from her cards but keeps her head down and moves a red queen to the black king.

"Nice move. I have this game on my computer. I'm amazing at it, so let me know if you need any help or anything, okay?"

"Sure. I think I'm all set, though."

"Okay, just speak up if you need a tip."

"I will."

"Roger that, over and out. Hey, do you ever call your dad Roger? Like do you ever say, 'Roger that, Roger'?"

"No." Her tone of voice is a little flatter than it would normally be. I think I'm starting to piss her off.

"Blackjack."

"What?"

"I don't mean blackjack. I mean black jack. Move the black jack to the red queen."

"Yeah, I know. I was going to. I just wanted to see if I could do anything else first."

"Okay. I don't think so, though."

"Thanks." Once again with the flat tone of voice. Nice.

I look out the window. There's nothing out there more entertaining than annoying Claire. "Hey, do you still play the flute?"

"No. Not really. I'm focusing on piano."

I hate the way she just said that, "focusing on piano." "How's that going? How's that piano focusing going?"

"Fine."

"Red seven on the black eight."

"I know."

"Do you think you're getting pretty good, or do you suck, or what's the story?"

"I wouldn't say I'm good, and I wouldn't say that I'm not good."

"So you're just pretty average, then? Just kind of in the middle?"

"Uh-huh." She deals out three cards from the deck.

"Ooh, black five."

"I know."

"Cool. Cool. Well, I'll let you play for a little while longer, and then I'll come back and annoy you some more."

She looks up at me and actually half smiles. "Okay, I can't wait."

I see the Vizquel girl all the time now. She looks so good in her bathing suit. She goes swimming by herself and sits outside her cottage by herself. Her mom mostly stays inside or goes to work somewhere. The car is gone now, so she must be at work. Mom told me the girl's name is Sophie. I want to do something. I want to meet her or say hi or something, but I don't know how to do that.

She's in the lake right now. I take a quart of fresh strawberries out of the fridge and walk it over to the Vizquels' cottage. I place it on the front step so she'll see it when she comes back from the lake.

I go back to our cottage and watch from the window as she walks up from the lake. She sees the strawberries and she picks them up. She looks around like she's wondering where they came from, but I don't think she can see me.

She takes them inside with her. I don't know what I was expecting. I guess I sort of wanted her to run over here and thank me and then we could meet, but I didn't leave her a note or anything, so I don't know why she would do that.

Mom and Dad are getting drunk with the Richardsons on their porch before dinner. Dad is having his third or fourth beer, and Mom is drinking wine coolers with Mrs. Richardson. I'm just sitting here with my headphones on, pretending to listen to my music, but with the sound turned way down so I can hear what they're saying.

Adults get really weird when they drink. Right now

Dad is talking louder and louder and laughing too long at nothing. Mom is dancing to the music on the radio. Motown.

Mom has this one dance move she always does when she gets a few wine coolers in her. She shifts her weight back and forth on her hips and snaps her fingers at the same time. Old people shouldn't be allowed to snap their fingers while they're dancing.

I turn my music up so I can get through the next two and a half minutes without puking. Finally, the stupid song ends and Mom sits down. They think I'm not listening, so I turn my music back down again.

All they're talking about is how the Sinister Minister is at it again. I guess he didn't just screw the lightbulb back in, like everyone thought he would. He installed some sort of metal grate in front of the lightbulb. Not only that, he installed this bell on the side of his cottage that rings every time his phone rings, so if he's on his dock, he can hear it.

Mr. Richardson is really angry about it. He keeps swearing like a crazy old man about the minister. He keeps calling him an SOB, which stands for "son of a bitch."

Dad says, "What I'd like to do . . . what I'd like to do . . ." When Dad drinks, it sometimes takes him a couple of tries to get through the sentence he started. "What I'd like to do is go over there in the middle of the night and cut the power to his whole damn area. I really would."

Mr. Richardson nods his head over and over. I feel bad for him that he's gotten so worked up. It's too bad. The minister's ruined his perfect world.

The only good thing about the minister problem is that the Richardsons keep inviting us over to hang out with them. It's like we're all of a sudden part of their family.

Dad is out in his kayak practicing his Eskimo roll. It looks really hard. He wants me to learn it too, so I wade out into the water and stand next to him while he gets ready.

He says, "Here's how we do it. I tip my body to the side, go under, and sweep my arm out like this." He gestures with his right shoulder, like he's throwing a punch. "Easy as pie, son."

I smile at him and nod. I disagree that it will be as easy as pie, but I don't feel like saying that. I disagree with the whole notion that pie is easy, actually. I don't have the first clue how to make pie. It's probably pretty complicated. There are probably a number of steps and ingredients. Every time I have ever tried to bake anything, it's always been a disaster, usually because I can never remember the difference between baking soda and baking powder.

Dad is getting ready for his first try. He says, "Here goes nothing." He dips his head to the side and the kayak rolls right over, but it doesn't come back up again. He's upside-down in the kayak. He makes some motion with his hands and the paddle, but the boat doesn't move at all.

I wonder if I should help him. He tries again, but it doesn't do anything. He's panicking, I think. He pulls himself out of the boat and I reach down underwater to grab his hand. I pull him up and he looks really disoriented. He shakes his head, opens his eyes wide, and spits some water out of his mouth.

"Whoa, that was intense," he says. "Did I come up at all?"

"No, not really."

"Not at all?"

"No. Sorry."

"Shit. You want to give it a try?"

It's always a good sign when Dad starts swearing around me. It means he's either drunk or really frustrated; either way, it's awesome.

I don't want to do this, but I say yes anyway. We flip the kayak right side up and then upside down to get all the water out. We go up onshore so I can get all the equipment on and so Dad can refer back to his book about how to do an Eskimo roll. Dad says, "See, son, it's a sweeping motion like this." He points to the picture of the guy in the book. I see what he means, but I can't really imagine myself doing that underwater. I get all the gear on and paddle out into the lake, turn the kayak around, and paddle back toward shore. Dad wades out into the lake and meets me about halfway up to his chest. He says, "If you get in trouble, just pull on this little loop." He shows me a loop of rope that will pull off the watertight seal, and then I'll be able to get out of the boat.

He holds the bow of the kayak and waits for me to set myself. I'm ready. I take a deep breath and lean over, but the boat doesn't tip right away. I take another breath and try again, but it won't go over. Maybe I'm not heavy enough.

Dad gives the kayak a little push and I go right over. I'm upside-down underwater, so the rocks and everything below me feel like they're above me. The sky is the floor, and the rocks are the sky. What am I supposed to do? Don't panic. Just push the paddle out.

Never mind that there's water going up my nose and I

can't do anything. I grab the release loop and pull and I'm out of the boat and swimming. I come up for air, and I can breathe again.

Okay, that was not a really supercool thing to do. Dad asks me if I want to try again, but I tell him I don't like being upside-down underwater and feeling like I'm going to drown.

I don't want to do that again. This is his thing, not mine.

Mom and Dad went into town this morning, so I'm hanging out on the beach with Mike's girlfriend, Eliza. Mike and Eliza are so cool. Especially Eliza, and not just because she's got huge tits. Really huge tits, actually. It's because she's got this amazing personality. She's a grown-up, but she's not grown-up at all. Not like my parents. She's just really wild and free. I hope when I'm a grown-up, I'll be like that.

Even with her tits, you know, she's just so cool about them. Like she's just hanging around in her bathing suit and she doesn't mind that I'm staring at them the whole time. She doesn't mind at all.

She's been coming down to the lake on the days when no one else is here. I guess she likes to be alone, but she doesn't seem to mind if I come over and talk with her while she's sunbathing.

Eliza's not afraid to ask anything either. That's the other thing I love about her. She says, "Are you still a virgin?"

"Me? Yeah, I guess."

"You guess? I think you would know."

"I am. I am, but I don't know if I'm going to be that much longer."

"Really? Do you have a girlfriend?"

"Yeah, yeah, but I'm not that into her."

Eliza laughs and reaches down to scratch her ankle. She's got a tattoo down there.

I say, "What about you?"

"What about me what?"

"Are you a virgin?"

She laughs again, kind of a smoky laugh that makes it sound like she's the furthest thing from a virgin. "No. I'm not a virgin. I wish I was, though."

"Really? I wish I wasn't."

Something about Eliza, she's like twenty-five, but she seems like a big teenager. I even feel like I've kind of got a shot with her. How cool would that be if she let me have sex with her? I would totally do that.

Eliza opens up another wine cooler and takes a big sip. Her lips are big and soft-looking. I'm getting a major hard-on. I can't help it.

"Do you want a sip?" she says.

"Yeah, sure." I reach out and take a drink of her wine cooler. It's really sweet and sparkly. I like it, but I don't really like it. I guess I'd rather have a Coke.

"You can have one if you think your parents wouldn't mind."

"Um, I don't know. They might mind a little. I don't know why."

"Okay, well, there's a Coke in the fridge if you want."

"Really? Cool." I get up and walk into the Richardsons' cottage. I love being in here. Everything is right where it should be, and there are all these pictures on the wall that make everything look so perfect.

I hope she didn't notice my boner when I stood up. Or maybe I don't care.

I open the ancient refrigerator and look for a Coke, but the only thing I see is Diet Coke. What the hell? This stuff is gross. At least it's cold, though.

I walk back out through the screen door and onto the stone patio. When I get rich, when I'm older, I'm going to buy this place from the Richardsons. I'll still let them come visit, but I'll live here year-round.

I sit down next to Eliza again and stare right at her tits. I wonder if she notices when I do that. Probably not. I'm pretty good at disguising it. I only look when I'm moving, or when they're moving, or when she looks away or something.

The best is when she reaches down to pick something up and I get to look right down her bikini.

Eliza said something, but I wasn't listening, so I just say, "Yeah."

"You do?"

"Yeah." I'm not sure what she's talking about, but it seems easiest to say "yeah."

"Really? You mind if I ask you a personal question?"

"Me? No. Go ahead."

"Oh, okay, because if you mind, I don't have to ask you."

"No, I really don't mind. I mean, I like it. I just didn't know that's what you were talking about." What am I talking about?

"Okay. So you don't have to answer if you don't want to, but I'm just curious, okay?"

"Yeah, sure."

"Has your . . . has your penis started to get bigger yet?"

I don't know what to say. That's not what I was expecting her to ask me, but it's also exactly what I'm in the mood to talk about.

"You mean right now?"

She laughs, but it wasn't a joke. "No. I mean like puberty. I'm just curious. When does a guy's penis start getting bigger?"

"Uh, I guess now. I guess it's getting bigger. I haven't measured or anything."

"You haven't? I thought all guys did that."

I have, but I didn't know other guys did too. I don't know if I can tell her that, though. Who cares? "Okay, I've measured it."

"You have? How big is it?"

"Uh, just like six inches."

She nods. "That's about normal."

"Really?"

"Oh yeah. I've known guys who were a lot smaller than that."

Okay, that's pretty good. I wonder if I should take it out right now and let her see it. I look around. No, we're in public. And plus, my parents got back a couple of minutes ago and they are probably wondering where I am.

I probably should go home, except I just want to do something crazy. I just want to show her what kind of a guy I am, in case she ever breaks up with Mike and wants to be with a guy like me.

I don't know. Anyway, Mom's calling me for lunch, so I guess I can't do anything right now. I head back to the cottage.

Anyway, with Eliza, I don't really know what I would do if things ever got really serious. I guess I'd just go with it. I don't know. It's not like being at a party and hooking up with some drunk eighth grader. I'd have to have some tricks up my sleeve or something. I should probably practice everything I'm going to do if I ever get a chance to do it.

I heard it's good to practice French-kissing by filling up a glass with ice cubes and then jiggling them around with your tongue for a while. Only thing is that gets pretty cold. I've made out with girls before, especially at parties, and it's not really like that. It's definitely not cold and hard. It's the opposite.

Like when we played spin the bottle in Eleanor's basement, and Janel Frenched all the guys. That was weird because her mouth was so much bigger than mine. I felt like I was getting swallowed whole. I hope it's not like that with Eliza.

Probably not. She's probably really good at everything. That's why I have to practice. But it's not like at home, where I can just lock myself in my room. Here I have to do it in the shower, and that sucks because there's only one bathroom and it's right next to the kitchen and living room and dining room, so everyone can hear everything. Besides, everyone is always trying to use the bathroom when I'm in the shower.

Eliza is down today again. I guess the washing machine at her house isn't working, so she needs to borrow the Richardsons'. I walk over and stand at the door of the garage, where the laundry is. I try and stand up straight so I can look really tall and good-looking.

Eliza turns around and sees me. "Hey, good-lookin'," she says.

"Hey." I should have said something about her body, about how amazing her body is. "Hey, big tits."

Oh shit. Maybe I shouldn't have said that. She turns

around with a really confused look on her face and then smiles and chuckles. I think I just got away with that. That was awesome.

She's wearing an outfit that you only wear when everything you own is dirty. A pair of ratty old sweatpants and a guy's tank top. Her tits are so huge they're basically spilling out of the sides of the tank top, and I don't even think she's wearing a bra, because her nipples are on high alert. Oh my God, she's got nice tits.

Eliza says, "So, what's going on?"

"Nothing. What's going on with you?"

Sometimes people ask you that question and the real reason they ask you is because they want you to ask them the same thing back. I think that's how Eliza is, because she just started talking before I even finished asking the question.

"My best friend, Amanda, from Boca Raton, called me last night. You'd love her. She's got an unbelievable body, like guys literally come up to her on the beach and ask her to model, but she doesn't do it, because she's Christian. Because I think . . . Anyway, I think they want her to do a spread or something and show some skin, and if I had her body, I'd do it in a second. So anyway, she called and she's got a boyfriend who's half Puerto Rican and half Dominican. Anyway, he's an amazing dancer, and he's also a cop. DEA, you know, Drug Encroachment Association or whatever. He was undercover with a bunch of Cubans who basically run the whole drug scene down there. . . ."

I've totally lost what she's supposed to be talking about, so I just look at her nipples through the tank top every time she gestures or moves or looks away. And every time she stops her story, I just nod and say, "Yeah." And then she keeps talking.

Eliza and I are going up to her house to hang out. I asked Mom and she said it was fine. Eliza drives a little two-door automatic with some rust on the driver's side. When I get a car, I want it to be a two-door. It's so sporty and cool.

Eliza drives with the windows open. I love doing that, but Mom never lets us. It's a lot more fun in a two-door car that's low to the ground anyway, instead of the Subaru.

Eliza steps on the gas and drives fast down the back road. I look over and check how fast we're going. Only seventy. It seems faster than that.

I reach my hand out of the window and feel the wind going through my fingers. I make my arm like a wave, and the air pushes it up and down.

I wonder what we'll do when we get to her house. Are we just going to get naked and screw on the carpet, or what?

Oh wait, I remember Eliza said that she and Mike have a water bed. That'll be fun.

We slow down and turn left onto a dirt road, somewhere outside of Interlaken. I'm kind of lost. This is the sticks out here.

Eliza and Mike's nearest neighbor is about a half mile away. I hope I don't have to go to the emergency room when I'm here. Eliza gets out of the car and walks into the house. She unlocks the door and goes into the house without holding the door open for me. I guess I wasn't really expecting her to have sex with me as soon as she opened the door. It doesn't matter. This is still fun.

91

I push my hair out of my eyes and look around the room. The light is coming in through a sliding glass door on the other side of the room, and I'm standing in the living room. Eliza turned down the hall and went I don't know where. The bathroom? The bedroom? Should I follow her?

There's a comfy-looking chair right in front of me. I don't think I've ever seen a chair like this. It's totally round with a big, fluffy cushion that looks like a pancake. I wonder if she and Mike have ever had sex on that thing.

Eliza comes back, goes into the kitchen, and heads straight to the refrigerator. I think she changed clothes, but she didn't change into anything sexy. She's wearing one of Mike's T-shirts and a pair of yellow workout shorts.

"Want a beer?"

"Uh, no thanks. Actually, sure."

"Okay." She opens a brown bottle and hands it to me, then grabs a wine cooler for herself. "Your parents wouldn't be mad, would they?"

"No, they're pretty cool." They're not at all cool, and I'm sure they would be pissed as shit if they knew what I was doing here, but who cares, it's not their life.

"Let's go out here." Eliza opens the sliding glass door and goes over and sits down in a lawn chair on the old brick patio. I sit down right across from her and try and look at her tits as I'm sitting. This new shirt covers up a lot more than the other one.

"This is really nice," I say. The yard is big, bigger than ours at home, and it's all mowed in perfect straight lines. I guess Mike gets that from his dad. This place is a lot crappier than his dad's house, though.

Eliza says, "So, do you get along with your parents?"

"Um, yeah, most of the time. I got in a big fight with my dad a few weeks ago."

"Really? What was it about?"

"It was just about something stupid. I wanted to go to the mall with this girl, and Dad wouldn't let me unless some adult came too. It was retarded."

"Hmm."

I can't tell if she wasn't listening or if she's thinking about what I was saying. I'm not really comfortable if I'm going to have to talk. I wish she would start talking again. Then I could ignore her and stare at her tits.

I look at her face instead. She's looking out at the yard, but she seems like she's looking at something really far away. It almost looks like she's going to cry or something. I don't get it. What did I say?

I say, "Did I say something?"

She pulls it back together. "Did you say something?"

"Yeah, I mean, are you okay?" I take a sip of my beer. It tastes like piss and water, but it's also good.

"No. Sorry, I was just thinking about something."

I try and think of all the things she could be thinking about, but the only thing I can come up with is that she's probably thinking about whether or not to have sex with me, but I really don't think that's it, because she looks really sad.

She takes a big sip of her wine cooler and then rests it on the plastic table between us. The table is wobbly, and it looks for a second like the bottle is going to tip over.

"I need to take a nap," she says, and stands up to go back into the house. She opens the sliding door and goes inside but turns around before she closes it again. "You can watch

TV or whatever until Mike gets home, and then maybe we can get him to take us out in the boat."

"Okay," I say, because I can't think of anything else to say.

"Oh, and there are some old copies of *Playboy* in the garage."

Wow, great. Now I really have something to do for a while.

Mike's garage is filled with stuff—not like his dad's garage—including his boat, but I think I can find the *Playboys* if I look hard enough. I'm actually pretty good at this sort of thing. I mean, my dad doesn't have a lot of this kind of stuff, but he has a few copies of *Playboy* hidden in the master bedroom. He used to keep them in his bedside table under a *National Geographic*, but then he moved them to his closet on the top shelf under the sweaters that he never wears.

I look around the garage, but there's nothing obvious like *National Geographic* or sweaters. This garage doesn't even have a floor, like cement or whatever—it's just dirt. My bare feet feel cold and dirty in here. Even though I've basically been barefoot all summer, this is one of the first times I've really noticed it.

There's a workbench with a bunch of old power tools, and at the end of the workbench there are two big cardboard boxes. The tops of the boxes are folded over, but they aren't taped or anything, so I just pull the first one open. Bingo.

This box is full of *Playboys*. Wow, I don't think I've ever seen this many magazines in one place. There must be two hundred or more in here. I want to go through them and see how far they go back, but I don't know when Mike is getting back, and I don't want him to find me in here with my shorts around my ankles.

I should probably get this over with. I grab the top magazine and flip it open to the centerfold. She's pretty hot. She's blond with big tits, like Eliza. She's from Arkansas. There's pictures of her washing a car in a barn with her top off. And pictures of her lying naked on a pile of hay.

I can imagine Eliza lying like that on a big pile of hay with her jean shorts open.

I walk back into the main part of the house and I can hear Eliza talking to someone. At first, I thought she was talking to someone in the house, but then I realized I was only hearing one half of a conversation and there were big spaces in what she was saying.

Her bedroom door is part open, but I can't quite hear all of the words. Her voice sounds angry, or not angry exactly, but more like really stressed out. I wonder who she's talking to.

I go down the hallway so I can hear the words a little better. "Do you think I don't know that? Do you think I don't know?"

Then there's a pause, like a fifteen-second pause. "I never said that. I never said I even wanted to."

Another long pause. "Of course. Of course I didn't. Are you asking me that? Are you seriously asking me what I think you're asking me?"

There's a man's voice on the other end of the line. Whoever he is, he's yelling through the phone. I can't understand a word he's saying, but he sounds pissed.

Eliza is quiet. Her voice gets soft, like she's trying to coo a baby back to sleep. "Mike. Mikey."

Oh. I wonder what they're fighting about. She goes on, "Mike, you know me. I would never do that. I would never do that to you. I love you. Don't you love me?"

A pause. Like a second. He must be saying that he loves her too.

Her voice gets lower and she whispers something that I can't hear and then giggles.

I want to get out of here. I want to go back home and hang out at the lake. This isn't what I thought I was getting into. This is annoying.

I go back into the living room and sit in the pancake chair. I want to get out of here. I want to disappear. I guess I'm just going to have to wait until Eliza drives me home.

I grab the remote and turn on the TV. I can't wait to get back to the lake.

We're going to the minor-league baseball game in Geneva. It's kind of a long drive, but it's something we do every year.

It's actually pretty cool. We park right next to the stadium and pay a couple of bucks and walk right in. We find seats on the third-base line with a whole bunch of regulars who give us a funny look because we're not wearing Geneva Cubs hats.

It's got that whole summer-baseball thing going on. Old-time baseball goodness. There's this kid walking around, probably not older than eight, with a voice louder than a heavy-metal singer's. He's just screaming the same thing over and over: "Pepsi. Popcorn. Peanuts and Cracker Jacks." Then he pauses like he forgot to say something and yells, "And lollies."

I always laugh when he does that, because it's the same way every year. Like he's always forgetting about the lollies.

"Dad, can I have a lolly?" I say it a little louder than I should, just to make myself laugh, but Dad thinks I'm trying to embarrass the kid, so he gives me the evil eye.

The kid turns around and walks the other way, back toward the first-base line. He'll be back. Maybe I'll get a lolly later. We already had dinner. We stopped at that old-style diner up on Route 13. The one where the waitresses actually come out to your car and ask you what you want. They must have thirty flavors of milk shakes there. I got butterscotch because I like those candies that old people eat, but it was gross.

A bunch of baseball players are already out on the field playing a game called pepper under a sign that says No Pepper. Dad explained it to me a long time ago. Three guys take turns throwing a baseball to a guy with a bat just a few feet away. And the guy with the bat has to bunt it back to them. It's fun to watch because the guys with the ball have a whole bunch of tricks, like throwing it behind their back or over their shoulder, trying to trick the guy with the bat.

They look like they're having a lot of fun out there. Makes me wish I were a baseball player. Dad buys a program and starts filling out all the different raffles and prizes and stuff. This is really the best part, because between every inning there's some crazy minor-league baseball stunt.

I scoot over to Dad and help him decide what names to put in what spaces. I want to win the Carvel ice cream cake, so I put my name there. Dad can do the One-in-a-Million Shot—where you try and throw a baseball through a hole from a hundred feet away, and if you do, you win like a hundred bucks or something.

Dad flips through the pages, and finally he gets to the Dizzy Bat competition.

I give Dad a look and then I look at Mom, and Dad gets the idea. He writes her name down on the piece of paper for the Dizzy Bat competition.

I can't wait until the seventh inning. That's when it's going to happen. This is going to be great.

Finally, it's the seventh inning. I already won the Carvel ice cream cake and Dad didn't get picked for the One-in-a-Million Shot. Some guy almost won a lobster by trying to catch a plastic lobster they shot out of a cannon toward center field, but he didn't catch it, so he didn't win.

The announcer comes on over the loudspeaker: "Ladies and gentlemen, may I please have your attention. Cathy Weeks, please come to the information booth under the grandstand." I don't think Mom has any idea what she's in for—I think she just thinks that she won something.

Mom is on the field, and her competitor in the Dizzy Bat competition is an eight-year-old boy. The ball boy is on the field explaining what she has to do—and she's laughing. They both have to put their head down on the end of a bat and spin around a bunch of times, until they get really dizzy, and then they have to run down the first-base line toward a pizza delivery guy. Whoever gets there first gets the pizza.

The kid is a lot shorter and probably has better balance, but Mom is so competitive, who knows what's going to happen?

The announcer tells them to start and Mom starts running in circles around her bat. She's getting dizzy already, I can tell, because she's starting to trip over her own feet. The little kid is running in circles and it doesn't seem to bother him. He's done with his circles and Mom is still working on hers. Dad is cheering and whistling, but I am just cracking up too much to even say anything.

Now the kid is trying to run down the baseline, but he's so dizzy he just keeps falling on his face.

Mom has finished her circles and is running down the baseline, but she's running sideways. I've never seen anyone run sideways before. She's looking where she wants to go, but she's having trouble figuring out how to make her body do it. Oh my God. That's the funniest-looking run I've ever seen.

The kid is back on his feet, but he still can't run. He must have twisted himself so fast that he really got out of balance. Mom is zigzagging down the baseline. She's about halfway to the pizza guy. She's getting her balance back and she's trying to straighten herself out, but now the kid is getting his balance back too. And the kid is much faster than Mom.

Mom is almost to the pizza guy, but the kid is picking up a lot of speed. The kid is sprinting and Mom is just kind of jogging to the finish line. I scream, "Go, Mom!"

Dad yells, "Go, Cathy!"

But the kid is too fast, and he reaches the finish line right before Mom does. They both collapse at the end, and the announcer comes on and says something about Sal's Pizza being the best pizza in town.

Oh well, that was kind of exciting. When Mom finally

makes her way back to us, we give her a hug and tell her, "Good job." She seems disappointed that she didn't win, but that's not the point. That was one of the funniest things I've ever seen, watching my mom compete against an eight-year-old in the Dizzy Bat competition.

We're having drinks on the Richardsons' porch, and the minister is piling seaweed into a small mountain on the beach.

Mr. Richardson takes a sip of his whiskey on the rocks and I can hear the ice cubes rattle inside the glass. He says, "The day he lights that seaweed . . ." He doesn't finish the sentence, but he pours himself another.

Dad says, "It was just a lump last week—now it's as big as your pile."

Mr. Richardson is just staring out through the screen. The women get up and go into the kitchen to get everyone some snacks. I sip my ginger ale and wiggle in the rocking chair. I'm waiting for someone to say something, but nobody does.

I got Mike and Eliza's phone number from Mrs. Richardson. I just want to give them a call and see if they're coming down in the boat anytime soon. I just think it would be cool to see them again and hang out like we did that one time.

I dial the number on the party line phone and wait for it to ring. I get nervous sometimes when I call people on the phone, especially girls, but I usually practice what I'm going to say before I call. This time I didn't do that, but I wish I had. I guess I'm just going to say hi and ask if Eliza is there. Hopefully, it'll be Eliza and I won't even have to ask.

"Hello." Shit, it's Mike.

"Hello, is Eliza there?"

There's a pause on the other end. I think it's maybe too long of a pause. He might be handing her the phone, or he might be waiting for me to say something else. Should I have said something else?

"Who the hell is this?"

Wow, he's really angry. I should have probably said who it was. I try and get it out, but I wasn't expecting him to be so angry. I start to say my name, but he's screaming into the phone so loud I have to hold it away from my ear. "Who the fuck is calling my house? Answer me!"

I didn't know he was going to be like that. I wouldn't have called if I'd known that.

I should hang up, but I'm afraid he'll just call me back. I say my name, but he doesn't hear me. He says, "What?"

I say, "Luke."

He pauses a long time and says, "Sorry, Luke, she's not here."

I try to say, "Okay, can you tell her I called?" but he's already hung up the phone. Did he find out about the *Playboy* or something? I hope not. I hope Eliza didn't tell him.

We all got up early so we could hike up to the waterfall. Mom's got her backpack filled with snacks. Dad has his camera.

I think we all just want to get away from the minister and the Richardsons and all of that shit. The old car is still there, except this year it looks like someone tried to set it on fire.

But it still feels magical here, even though there's hardly

any water in the creek this year. I just want to feel the way I did when I was little. When I was in awe of everything.

I still love the feeling of getting closer to the waterfall. The walls of the gorge rising up as we walk. The sound of the water. It starts like a hum in the distance, and then it keeps getting louder until it's roaring right in our faces. But there's just not that much water in the creek this year, so all the rocks are bleached white and covered in dried seaweed and we can't hear the water yet. We wind around the final turns. We're almost there and I'm excited.

We turn the last corner, and I see the waterfall, but I also see Sophie standing underneath the water, letting it rain over her shoulders.

I've never been here when there was anyone else here. It's weird having someone else here. It's like she knows our secret.

We walk over to the other side of the waterfall so we don't bother her. I could swim in the little pool, but it's probably cold. I could get near her, but I've never talked to her before, so it would be strange to start now.

She sees us and smiles. I think she's smiling at me, but she could be smiling at my parents. I nod back, but I don't know if she is paying attention. Dad calls out, "Hello!" Why does he have to be so loud?

She's got this long black hair that looks so pretty when it's wet. It comes all the way down her back. And her eyes, she's got these huge eyes. They look like cats' eyes. I wish I could think of something to say to her.

I throw a stone at the shale wall, so it comes down in a mini avalanche. This feels so awkward. I don't know what we're doing here. There's nothing to do if we can't stand under the water.

Dad says, "Climb up there. I'll take your picture." I know what he means. He wants to take a picture just like the one from last year that's on our fridge.

I take a step up onto a small ledge on the side of the waterfall, but the shale doesn't hold under my weight like it used to. My feet slip and I have to grab a plant by the roots to keep from falling back. I stand up straight and say, "Here?"

"No, a little higher."

I turn around and climb a little higher. This seemed so easy when I was smaller. I get high enough so that he can't complain that I'm not high enough.

"Okay, now put your arms up like you did before."

I do what he says and he takes the picture. I can see Sophie looking at me. I know it's not going to be as good as the first picture. Nothing is as good as it used to be.

There's a little bit of rushing water toward the top of the waterfall. I could keep climbing up there and put my head under the water. The cliff isn't that steep—it's just wet and slippery. I can climb it.

I put my hand on a piece of rock and work my way up onto the first wide ledge. I slide across to my left, up the slippery stone. I've got a good hold on the rock, so I can keep myself from falling down.

My feet want to slip, but I'm holding myself up with my arms. I'm strong enough to hold myself up with just my arms. I reach up to the next ledge and I pull myself up. I'm getting pretty high up here. I'm not sure how I'm going to make it down without slipping.

Mom says, "Are you sure it's safe?" She sounds worried.

"I'm sure."

I glance down at the rocks below. If I fall, it's going to really hurt. My parents are watching. Sophie is watching. I climb higher. I'm up to the next ledge.

There's a spot where the water has carved a natural bathtub in the stone. This is so cool. It's like a little hot tub, except the water is cold, but it shoots in from above and spills out below. This is the coolest thing I've ever seen.

I step into the bathtub and put my feet over the edge. My parents can't see me anymore. I'm alone up here. Dad calls out, "Son! Are you okay?"

"I'm fine."

"Are you coming down?"

"I guess." I could sit up here forever, but I won't. I should go down. I'm going to go down the opposite way I came up. There are all these little ledges I can climb down, even though they look slippery.

I have to hold on to the shale to make my way down the side of the waterfall. I don't know if I should face the wall or just put my butt down and try and sort of slide down. That'll look stupid. I can't see if Sophie is still down there.

The water is making it hard to get a good grip on the wall. Plus the shale is pretty crumbly. I'm trying to hold on. This is like man against nature. I just have to hold on. I think I can hold on, but my grip is slipping.

My hands are wet and the shale is starting to pull out of the waterfall, but I can't let go, because I'll slide right down. I don't want to fall down the waterfall. Oh shit, my hands are slipping. I don't want to do this. I don't want this.

Shit. I'm slipping. I'm falling. I can hear my mother

screaming. Oh shit, I'm falling. I hit the rock hard with my back and put my arms down to try and slow myself. I'm still sliding, and my arms are getting all cut up. I flip myself onto my stomach and try to stop myself with my knees and fingernails.

I hit the water. Mom and Dad are running over to me, but I call out, "I'm okay. I'm okay."

I think I cut myself. I think I cut myself on some of the stone.

Oh God, I've got a big cut on my knee from where it scraped across the stone. Mom is bending over me. "Are you okay?"

"Yeah."

"Thank God."

I look around for Sophie, but she's gone. I wonder if she saw me fall. Maybe she'll want to help.

Dad helps me stand up, but the cut on my knee is bleeding all the way down my shin. It hurts to walk on. I can't walk.

Dad puts himself under one arm. That makes it a lot easier to walk. I can hop on my good leg and keep the other one up.

Dad says, "That was pretty stupid."

"Yeah," I say.

My back is really hurting too. I think I scraped it pretty good. My butt too. My whole body is hurting now. I ripped a hole in the back of my bathing suit. That's embarrassing.

I hop along as far as I can, but my body is aching so much. Mom puts herself under the other arm, and even though she's a lot shorter than me, they carry me home.

The doctor at the emergency room gives me a bunch of shots, pulls the little pieces of shale out of my cuts, and stitches me up.

Mom and Dad went to the hospital gift shop and bought

me a bunch of magazines and some puzzle books to look at while I'm recovering.

They take me home and set me up on the green couch. My leg is still throbbing, and I'm just plain tired.

Mom and Dad leave me alone for a while and go down to the lake, and I close my eyes.

I wonder where Sophie went. Her eyes look like an Egyptian queen's eyes. They're huge and brown, and I don't know why, but I want to stare into them for as long as I can.

Mom wakes me up. She's holding a peach. Mom says, "I think this is for you."

"What?"

"Someone left it outside the front door while you were sleeping."

"Oh."

"Do you know who left it?"

"No."

"You didn't see anyone?"

"No. I was asleep."

"Hmm. That's a mystery. You would think they would leave a note."

"Yeah, I guess they just wanted me to have a peach."

The Richardsons brought over the newspaper so I would have something new to read.

I'd like to read a story about someone bringing a peach to someone who fell down a waterfall.

The whole Richardson clan is down for the weekend and I'm missing it. Mike and Eliza, Joe and Danielle, even Mary, and they're all out on the lawn playing soccer. I want to go out and play so bad. They look like they're having the best time. The minister's van is gone and my parents and the Richardsons are having drinks on the porch.

I limp out onto the lawn and stand next to the field. Joe and Mary are on one team, and Mike, Eliza, and Danielle are on the other. It's not really fair because Mary and Joe are both really good. They can pass and dribble and do everything. They've got two orange cones set up on either side of the lawn for the goals, but they don't have a goalie.

"Can I be goalie?" I say it loud enough so everyone can hear it, but they ignore me. I say it again and this time they all stop and think about it. I hope Mike doesn't say anything about that weird phone call or the *Playboy*.

Mike says, "Sure, if you feel up to it."

Eliza smiles at me. "Watch out, you guys. This kid's dangerous." I wish she hadn't called me "kid."

I go out to the middle of the goal that Mike and the ladies are going to shoot on. This way it's three on three and it's more fair, and besides, I want to be on the winning team.

Joe passes the ball to Mary and she makes a nice little move to go right around Eliza. I don't think Eliza has ever played soccer before. Danielle tries to get in front of Mary, but Mary goes right by her too. Danielle stuck her foot out and Mary had to kick the ball a little farther away than she wanted to. Mike comes running in and steals the ball from her.

Mike is better than I thought he was. He makes a sweet crossover move and goes right past Joe. Okay, here he comes. He's going to shoot. Which way? He kicks it really hard. Which way? Left? No, right. Shit.

Fuck, I fell on my knee. Fuck that hurts. Ow. Fuck, I think I hurt my knee again. That was so fucking stupid.

Ah shit. It's bleeding. It's bleeding a lot. Fuck. It looks like we're heading back to the emergency room.

It's the same doctor as the last time I was here. And last time he was really nice. He was making jokes about boys doing stupid stuff while he was pulling the little pieces of stone out of my knee, but this time he's in a really bad mood. He says I popped open almost all of my stitches when I fell down on my knee.

I notice that he didn't give me any painkillers this time. He's probably pissed off because he has to do this all over again. It really hurts every time he puts a stitch in. It really does. Like a needle being pulled in and out of my knee. I don't get why he's so mad. He's probably going to make more money off of me. I wonder if they get paid per stitch or if they get paid by the amount of time they take with each patient or what.

I don't know, but if he gets paid by the hour, he should really slow down, because he's not being very careful this time.

The first time he did this, I think he took about twice as much time. Finally, he finishes with his stitches and then takes Mom outside the room to talk.

I'm practicing my rock skipping on the beach because it's about the only thing I can do without hurting my knee again. The Richardsons are working on their gardening, and the minister is adding to his seaweed pile.

The minister goes back to the shed on the other side of

his house. He brings back a gallon of gas in one of the red plastic containers like we have. Not like the nice metal ones Mr. Richardson has.

He pours a little of it over the seaweed and lights it on fire. There's not a lot of flame, but there is a lot of dark gray smoke. And the smoke is blowing right off the beach into Mr. and Mrs. Richardson's bedroom window. I don't know how well that's going to go over. Probably not too well.

Seaweed doesn't smell good when it's burned. It's got this really nasty, ashy smell and the smoke hurts my eyes. It almost smells like burning hair, but not as bad.

Mr. Richardson is gardening on the other side of the house, so it takes a while for the smoke to get over to him.

He doesn't waste a second. He walks right over to the minister and starts talking. I can't hear what he's saying, but I don't have to. I can see exactly what he's saying.

Mr. Richardson stops talking and the minister starts. I can't hear what he's saying either, but he's speaking without moving any other part of his body. Mr. Richardson shoves his hands way down into his pockets and keeps them there.

He doesn't listen for too long. He turns around and walks back to his yard. In a way, the whole thing is kind of funny, watching two old guys argue with each other.

I call out, "Hey, Mr. Richardson, what did you say to him?"

Mr. Richardson just ignores me and keeps on walking. That's not a good sign.

The wind shifts after dinner. A north wind, blowing right up the beach and toward the minister's cottage. Mr. Richardson doesn't waste any time. He goes right to the garage and gets his antique gas can, douses his stick pile, and lights it up. It's our last night. I'm glad I got to see this.

The flames rise up into the fading light, and the smoke drifts across the lawn toward the minister's house. If this were a James Bond movie, he'd say something like "Looks like the *wind* has shifted," putting the emphasis on "wind" and making it seem like that actually meant something else.

From the picnic table, I just watch the smoke cross the yard and go right into the minister's windows. There are lights on in there, but I'm not sure anyone is home.

The minister drives a big white van with a cross painted on the side in red. Not like the Red Cross, but a Jesus cross painted red. The van is still in the driveway, but I don't see him.

The Richardsons invite us over to have marshmallows around their bonfire, and we carry our folding chairs onto their beach and sit down.

Mr. Richardson hands me a stick and two marshmallows and I get to work. I like to toast my marshmallows slowly on the edges of the flames, constantly spinning the stick so they cook evenly. I watch them, so if one of the marshmallows catches on fire, I'm ready for it and can blow out the flame before it gets too charred. It takes a while to cook them this way, but finally they're done and I take them out of the fire.

I look around the fire at everyone's faces: Mom and Dad, Mr. and Mrs. Richardson, Mike, Joe, Mary, Danielle, and Eliza. They stare at the flames like they're hypnotized. Their faces are orange and flickering. A rock pops inside the fire and everybody snaps out of it. I want to say something to liven things up and get everyone to stop thinking so much, so I start singing a song from a CD we used to have in the car when I was little.

> Down by the bay, where the water-
> melons grow,
> Back to my home, I dare not go,
> For if I do, my mother will say . . .

And then you make up two rhyming things, like:

> Did you ever see a bear combing
> his hair
> Down by the bay?

It takes a second for everyone to pick up on my song, but halfway through the third verse, Mr. Richardson still hasn't chimed in. He's just staring into the flames.

> . . . my mother will say . . .

I say, "Mr. Richardson, take it."

He looks up. "What?" He wasn't listening. I wonder what he was thinking about.

I take it:

> Did you ever see a bee with a sun-
> burned knee
> Down by the bay?

We keep singing for a while, until we run out of marsh-mallows and the fire dies in the stones. We walk back to our cottage, through the Richardsons' yard. The minister's van isn't there anymore.

We leave today, but we're taking our time. We're going to have one last breakfast at the picnic table. Dad made pancakes and used up as much of the groceries as he could. Whatever we don't eat we can give to the Richardsons.

I carry the syrup and the carton of milk. Dad carries the pancakes and the coffee. Mom's got the glasses for milk and a small container of strawberries. Dad joked about putting peppermint stick ice cream on his pancakes. Actually, I'm not sure if he was joking.

We all sit down on the lake-watching side of the picnic table. I start cutting up my pancakes so I can get as much syrup on them as possible. I'm ready for people to start saying "serene."

"What the fuck is that?"

I look up expecting to see a sniper. Dad's looking out to the water, toward the Bells' dock. I don't see what he's looking at.

Oh wait. I see it. There's a new flag flying at the end of the dock. A Confederate flag.

Mom picks up her plate and stomps back into the cottage. Dad and I follow her with the rest of the food.

She says, "The Sinister Minister has gone too far this time. Doesn't he know where he is? This is the North, not the South. Where does he think he is? He put a Confederate flag up at the end of his dock. It just makes me so mad to look at it. Who does he think he is? This isn't Alabama or Georgia."

My mom is really mad. I've never seen her this mad.

She's stomping around the cottage, packing up our stuff and throwing it in the suitcases.

She says, "I mean, the nerve. The nerve! He's just . . . he's just . . . I don't know. I do not know what he's thinking. That man is a terrible person."

My parents grew up in the sixties. They marched against the Vietnam War. They protested segregation, and now, all these years later, there's a flag up, promoting all the things they protested, right in their backyard.

Dad is mad too. He's pacing around the cottage. Dad says, "That son of a bitch is going to have to take that damn thing down. That is not going to stand. That thing is going to have to come down."

Mom and Dad are in the car. They didn't want to come down to the beach to say good-bye to the lake. This has been the worst two weeks of my life. Everything bad has happened.

I wish I could go back in time and change everything. I wish I could keep that stupid minister from moving into our neighborhood. Everything changed when he moved in.

I wish I could go forward in time too. And be a few years older so Eliza wouldn't look at me like I'm a little kid. I wish I'd never gone up to her house.

I limp down to the Richardsons' dock, stand in the sun, and look at the water. I love how it changes every day. Sometimes it's as smooth as glass, sometimes it looks like a mirror, and sometimes it's choppy as hell.

Right now it's just a little wavy. The waves lap up against the dock, and the sound makes me relax a little. The water is so perfect.

I close my eyes and listen to the waves lapping up against the dock and feel the warm wind coming from the south.

I wish I could live here. I wish I could live here forever, just like this, except for without the Confederate flag.

We're in the car and we're pulling away. The pine branches scrape against the kayak and Dad cringes. I look back over my shoulder at the Confederate flag blowing in the wind at the end of the Bells' dock.

Dad says, "That thing better be gone by the time we get back next year. It better be gone or I don't know what I'll do."

15

"Would you boys like some ice cream?" Dad sounds stupid. We all know he just wants to stop and get his peppermint stick.

My best friend, Steve, is in the backseat with me. I've been telling him about this place ever since we were little, and he's finally going to get to see it for himself. I show him the Wirth mansion and the house where the famous guy from TV used to live. He takes out one of his earbuds but leaves the other one in.

I say, "That farm stand has the best corn on the cob, and really good fresh strawberries too."

He just looks out the window and nods.

I tell him about the luckystones and the old farm they turned into a winery. It's kind of cool having somebody from home come up here, but I'm not sure he's really getting it.

Like when I pointed out the power station with the two smokestacks pumping all of that smoke out. I know it's pollution and everything, but it's kind of beautiful too in a weird way. He just said, "That's really bad."

But we're going to have an awesome time this year. This is the first time I've ever gotten to bring a friend with me. I told my parents I wasn't going to come unless I could bring Steve. They only agreed after they talked to his mom and found out about all the stuff that's been going on with him at school ever since his parents got divorced. They all agreed it would be good for both of us if he came up here. We pull down the gravel driveway and the tree scrapes the top of the car. Our cottage looks smaller and crappier than ever.

Steve and I walk down to the beach. He sees the Confederate flag first. I was hoping it would be gone.

He says, "Is that yours?"

"No," I say, and start looking for skipping stones. I pick up the first flat stone I see and it comes out of my hand at exactly the right angle. It skips like a dream across the water and out toward the buoy. It must have skipped twenty times.

I pick up another stone. This one is totally flat and smooth and thin, just like a playing card. I skip it, but it's too perfect and it just knifes into the water. I can never get a perfect stone to skip.

Steve skips one and it's a beauty. It goes out and skips about a thousand times toward the minister's dock. I say, "Nice one."

I haven't seen the minister yet, but his dogs are here, roaming around the Richardsons' lawn looking for a spot to take a shit they haven't already used.

I see Mr. Richardson in his cottage watching them through the living room window. He's holding something in his hand. It looks like a stick. I wonder if he's going to come out and start hitting those dogs. I squint to see if I can tell what it is Mr. Richardson is holding.

Is that a rifle? It looks like it, the way he's holding it. It looks heavy and solid. I wonder if he's going to shoot the minister's dogs.

The ugly brown dog squats right in the middle of Mr. Richardson's yard and starts taking a big shit. I look back at Mr. Richardson, but he's not standing in the window anymore. He's coming out of the house with that thing he's carrying. Jesus, is he going to shoot it?

Mr. Richardson comes out of the house and points toward the dog with the thing in his hand. It's not a rifle, but I can't tell what it is because of the way he's holding it.

The dog never sees it coming but yelps like a puppy and goes down. I didn't hear a gunshot, but there's a big red spot on the back leg of the dog. He shot it with a paintball gun. It's not blood, it's paint.

The dog gets up and limps back across the yard toward the minister's house.

Mr. Richardson watches the dog for a minute and then puts his paintball gun in the garage. He comes out with one of his antique lacrosse sticks.

He walks right up to the pile of steaming shit in his yard and pokes at it. He picks up the shit with the lacrosse stick. He cradles it for a second, then throws across his body, and the dog shit flies about thirty-five feet and lands right on the minister's front step.

I have to bite my lip to keep from laughing out loud. I can tell by the way Mr. Richardson walks over to the hose and cleans off the lacrosse stick that this isn't the first time he's done this.

I wish I had a camera. I would have loved to take a picture of Mr. Richardson flipping shit across the yard with an antique lacrosse stick. That's not something you see every day.

Steve has been standing next to me this whole time and hasn't said anything. I look up at him to see what his reaction is to all of this. He lifts his eyebrows and twists his face in that way that he does when he's about to say something funny and then says, "Pretty sweet vacation spot, dude."

Steve and I are sitting at the picnic table whittling sticks into supersharp points, because we're going to have a campfire at some point and we'll use them to roast marshmallows on.

Steve's talking about one of our friends back home. "Derek is such a dick, dude."

"I know."

"Did I tell you? He was standing in the hallway on the last day of school, and my little sister was there. Did I tell you about that, dude?"

"Wait, what happened?"

"Derek was standing there like a dick, like he always does. And my little sister was helping me take my stuff out of my locker, and anyway, Jim, Mike, Dan, and I paid her two bucks to go up to Derek and tell him that she hates him."

Steve's little sister is only ten, and she's actually really cute and sweet, so I'm kind of surprised she did that.

I say, "Really?"

"Yeah, dude. It was hilarious."

"What did Derek do?"

Steve laughs. "He just made that face." He scrunches up his face and changes his voice so it's really obnoxious and says, "You guys are dicks."

I laugh, but it doesn't really seem all that funny to me. Steve is super sarcastic all the time, and usually that's what I like about him, but up here it doesn't quite fit.

Sophie Vizquel walks past us to take a swim. Jesus, when did she grow up? She's always been pretty, but now she has this body that's like very grown-up.

When she gets far enough away so that she can't hear, Steve says, "Wow. You didn't tell me about her."

"Yeah, she's hot."

"Dude, she's fucking insanely hot. I'm going to go rub one out right now."

Steve gets up and goes into the cottage. Okay, gross.

I sort of wish Sophie and I had talked or played together when we were kids so that it wouldn't be so awkward to talk to her now. I did that thing where I gave her fruit last year, but that seems so lame now.

I don't know. I wonder if I should do that again. I go into the cottage, check to make sure Steve's still in the bathroom, and look in the fridge. Mom and Dad are usually good about buying a lot of fruit when we're here. Let's see, we've got a quart of strawberries. We've got some fresh raspberries too. Raspberries would be good.

I take them over to her house while she's in the water and leave them on her front step and run back over to our cottage.

I hope nobody saw me, especially Steve. He would think that was a Derek move.

Steve and I are playing soccer in the Richardsons' yard. They've got this big old tree and a telephone pole about eight feet apart that they hang a clothesline from. It makes the perfect soccer goal.

Steve and I take turns shooting and being goalie. He's a better goalie than I am because he's taller, but I'm a better shot, so it's a good matchup. He's really good at leaping to his left to get the balls I shoot up in that direction, so I keep trying to shoot the ball through the upper right corner, but I keep hooking it, so it just winds up in the center and he stops it easily.

My problem is I'm not getting enough power on my kicks. This time I'm going to lean down and nail the shit out of the ball. Steve is up on his tiptoes, ready to leap.

I lean over the ball and come up on it with all my weight and slam through the ball with the laces of my shoe. I nailed it, but oh shit. I hit it too high. It flies over Steve and the goal and right into the Richardsons' bedroom window.

"Oh shit," I say, and Steve turns and looks at me with his eyes wide open.

I run over to the window and see if there's any broken glass there. Thank God, there's no broken glass, but the screen is popped out on one side. Oh well, no problem. I'll just slap that back in there.

It doesn't want to go back in all the way, but that's okay. No one's going to notice. It's fine.

My mom told me that Eliza and Mike got married over the winter when we weren't here. Plus, they had a baby, so I guess things are kind of busy up at their house. Damn, I was sort of hoping to hang out with Eliza more this summer.

I also wish she'd invited me to the wedding, but who cares—it's not like we're really that good friends. Mrs. Richardson said it was a small wedding anyway, just family.

I haven't seen pictures of the wedding, but I saw some

pictures of the kid. Her name is Emma, and she's already five months old. Pretty cute, I guess, but all babies look alike to me.

Mr. Richardson comes over to us when we're eating dinner at the picnic table. He looks pissed, but he always looks a little pissed.

"Did one of you . . ." He pauses. "Did one of you kick something through my window?"

Dad and Mom look at me and Steve, and Steve looks at me. Shit. Nobody says anything. I feel like everybody just pushed me out on a branch and started sawing.

Fuck, I hate having to admit to shit. "What do you mean?" I say.

"Someone kicked a ball or something through my window. Ripped up one of my copper screens."

Shit. Copper. That sounds expensive. Everyone already knows it was me who did it, so I might as well admit it. "Yeah, Mr. Richardson. I'm sorry. I didn't know that it had done any damage. I'm really sorry."

He stands there for a second and then turns around and walks back toward his cottage.

I call after him, "Do you want me to see if I can fix it or something?"

He turns around in the middle of his perfect lawn and says, "No, thank you, you've done enough." We all watch him walk back to his cottage.

Finally, Dad says, "I guess you guys should be more careful where you play, huh?"

Steve says, "Is it just me or did he kind of freak out on you?"

I say, "No, I messed up. I should have told him about it."

Mom nods. She always likes it when I learn my lesson.

Jesus, that was kind of harsh, though. I mean, I know I fucked up his screen, but I did apologize too. It doesn't seem so bad that he couldn't have at least accepted my apology.

It's a full moon. We're sitting on the beach, trying to look at the stars, but all my parents can look at is the Confederate flag flapping in the breeze. Dad is really pissed about it all over again. He can't let it go. I can let it go because I don't care that much, but he and Mom can't take their eyes off it.

Dad keeps swearing under his breath, and Mom has this real tense look on her face. Nobody is having any fun. Steve is listening to music, which isn't what you're supposed to do out here. We can all hear the bass through his headphones. This sucks.

I say, "If it bothers you so much, why don't you just go and take it down?"

Dad looks over at me and says, "Yeah, you're right." He stands up and walks onto the dock and all the way down to the flag. This isn't like him. This isn't something he would do, but he's doing it.

He unwraps the rope, lowers the flag, unhooks it from the rope, and folds it neatly on the dock. Mom says, "Oh no."

Dad walks back down the dock toward us with a satisfaction I've never seen. He's smiling, and his crooked teeth catch the light from the moon.

Steve takes off his headphones and says, "What's going on?"

I say, "I'll explain it to you later."

Dad sits back down and I say, "Awesome."

Mom says, "Don't encourage him."

Dad says, "I'll write him a letter tomorrow and explain why I took it down."

It's back up. I woke up this morning feeling pretty good about what Dad did last night, because I thought it was over, but it's not over. The stupid flag is back up, just like nothing ever happened. And what's worse, now there is a sign on the minister's dock, in red paint that's still wet, that says No Tres Passing. He's a fucking idiot. He wrote "trespassing" like it was two words. The French translation would be "No Very Passing."

The four of us are sitting at the picnic table. Mom and Dad and Steve are drinking coffee, and Mom heated up one of those frozen coffee cakes. I don't like coffee, but I like coffee cake. No one's talking and Steve has his headphones on. Mom and Dad are just staring out at the lake.

I hear a dog whimper like someone kicked it. And then the sound of a sliding glass door opening. The minister is coming out of his house. Oh shit, he's walking right toward us. His piece-of-shit dogs are following him, like they're his gang and he's coming for a fight.

Mom and Dad and Steve and I all stand up, shoulder to shoulder, like we're ready to fight too. Dad moves over in front of Mom. I can't believe this is happening.

The minister comes to about six feet from us and stands there with his hands on his hips. He looks like a polar bear in a black suit. I thought he would come closer. He says, "Don't appreciate y'all trespassing on my property."

Dad says, "Yeah, well, we don't appreciate your flag."

"My flag is my business, and this is my beach."

Mom says, "No, it's a right-of-way. It's in our deed."

"It's my beach. It's my property, and I don't appreciate y'all trespassing. Y'all don't cease and desist, I'm going to call the police."

Dad says, "You can't do that."

"Watch me." He turns around and starts walking back to his house.

Mom calls after him, "You should take down that flag!"

He turns and yells back, "I'm from West Virginia!"

Steve and I are sitting on the couch. He's trying to get cell phone reception so he can call his girlfriend. Mom and Dad are pacing around the cottage. She says, "Doesn't he know that West Virginia wasn't even part of the Confederacy? Virginia was, but West Virginia split off precisely because they didn't want to be part of the secession." That's exactly like her. She never misses a chance for a teaching moment.

I say, "I don't think he cares."

"Well, he should care."

Dad is angry too. He's stomping back and forth, acting like he's a tough guy and he might at any moment go over there and beat up the minister. We all know he won't do that. He says, "I'm tempted to . . ." He bites his lip, like he can't believe the amount of anger that's inside of him. "I'm tempted to write him a letter."

I laugh out loud and everyone looks at me like I just farted in front of the queen of England. "Sorry," I say, but it is kind of funny how mad they both are and how the only solution they can come up with is to write him a letter.

Everyone is annoying me. Especially Steve. I was going to take him up to the waterfall with me, but I just don't think he'd appreciate it. I tell everyone I'm going for a walk, but I don't tell them where I'm walking to.

I go out the driveway and up the road to the top of the hill, where the old graveyard is, and cut through the barley field to the trail that goes down the gorge. This is the faster way to go.

It sort of takes the fun out of it, going down the trail instead of walking up the creek bed, but it just takes so long that way.

There's not as much anticipation this way. Not the same is-the-waterfall-here-or-is-it-around-the-next-corner, heart-in-my-throat, I-hope-there's-a-lot-of-water kind of thing. It's just, go down the trail, turn the corner, try not to slip on the slippery rocks, and I'm here.

I guess there's a pretty good amount of water this year. It's not the best and it's not the worst. It's in the middle.

I take off my socks and shoes, sit at the edge of the pool, and let the minnows nibble at my toes for a while. There are butterflies swirling around a bush on the gorge wall, and the water and the air mixing together makes me happy.

I don't feel really happy, but happy enough, I guess. Happy in a sad way. Melancholy, is that the word for it? Happy that I'm here and happy that the waterfall is still here, but kind of sad that I don't feel the way I used to about it.

The adults have decided to throw themselves a party tonight, just to raise a little hell and get under the minister's skin. Mr. and Mrs. Richardson and my parents' friends Roger and Kay and Norm and Bonnie are all coming. Dad went to the supermarket and bought so much beer. I haven't seen that much beer anywhere except for in a supermarket.

Norm is kind of the main party planner, because he just really likes to party. He's bringing his sound system, which should be interesting, and he is also planning a few "surprises," according to Dad. I don't know what that means.

The Richardsons are letting us use their parking area for the party, partially because they hate the minister and partially because they just want to make sure the party isn't going to spill out onto their lawn too much.

Steve and I don't really have anything to do. It's not our party. We're not even invited really, so we open up the garage door and put out a couple of lawn chairs and sit down to watch the show.

Norm is dressed up as Elvis. He's in the full costume, with the wig and the jumpsuit and a giant pair of gold sunglasses. He keeps saying "Hey, baby" in this weak Elvis impression.

Dad is wearing his beer helmet from his fortieth-birthday party. It's a novelty hat that he puts two beers in, and then a couple of tubes come down from the beers into his mouth. I guess that's the quickest way to get drunk, because he's already dancing around in a way that's hard to watch.

Norm's sound system is even louder than I thought it would be. He's blasting oldies, and he and Dad are dancing together like a couple of fags. This would be too embarrassing to watch, except now it's so bizarre I can't stop watching.

Steve stands up and goes to the back of the garage. He comes back with a beer in each hand. He hands me one and opens one for himself.

"Where did you get that?"

"I stole them from the cooler."

"Nice." I open my beer and take a gulp. It tastes like crap, but as long as I get a little buzzed, it'll be fine.

The adults are listening to Motown and dancing in the dark on the driveway. Norm goes over and turns on the headlights in his truck and then goes around to all the other cars and turns the headlights on in all of them too. All the headlights are focused on the minister's house, and I don't think that's an accident.

Steve chugs his beer and gets us both another one. Motown is pretty good music, especially when you've had a beer. All of the adults are dancing around in the headlights now, and they're casting these gigantic shadows across the lawn and onto the minister's house. Even the Richardsons are out there dancing. I never thought I'd see that.

They turn the music up even louder, and Norm starts stripping out of his Elvis costume. Bonnie's helping him. Gross.

Steve stands up and chugs his beer, and I do too, because what else are we going to do?

Steve walks over and starts going through all the paint and crap at the back of the garage.

He says, "Let's fuck something up."

"Like what?"

"I don't know. Want to make a cross and burn it on the minister's lawn?"

I hope he's joking. "Nah, let's fuck something else up."

Steve doesn't say anything. He goes through an old box filled with screws, dead fuses, and mousetraps, until he finds an old bottle of bleach. That's awesome. That's perfect. This is going to be hilarious.

We saw this prank on *Jackass* one time, where they bleached somebody's yard and made a bunch of fucked-up designs and shit. It was hilarious because the grass all died in the pattern of the designs and the guy who lived there got really mad.

We take the bottle of bleach and walk around the back of the cottage. Everyone is on the other side, drinking, dancing, and singing along to the music. I would do it right here on our little patch of lawn, but I'm afraid they'd figure out that it was us.

I motion for Steve to follow me, and we slip down into the creek. I'm the master of figuring out ways around my parents. We jump out of the creek on the other side of the Richardsons' garage and run around the back of the house to the woodpile, where the Richardsons' and the minister's yards meet. I can hear my dad and Norm singing "My Girl" together, but luckily I can't see them. I hope I don't act like that when I get old.

I was thinking that we'd do this on the minister's yard, but his is really patchy and dead anyway. I don't think he'd even be able to tell.

Steve squats down behind a tree. The Richardsons' yard is so green and spongy. I say, "You want to just do it here?"

"Sure."

On the show, I think the guy drew a big cock and balls, but that's too complicated. I'm trying to think of something that's simple and also doesn't right away say "Teenagers did this."

I know, a big cross. That way Mr. Richardson will think the minister did it. Besides, he already hates the minister anyway; it's not like they're going to become best friends.

I whisper to Steve what I want to do and make the symbol of a cross on my chest like a Catholic. He nods. He takes the cap off the bleach bottle and runs with it across the yard in a straight line. This is going to be awesome.

I show him where the second line should go, and he pours that too and then goes over both lines a few more times, until the bleach is all gone. The music is still playing and I can hear my parents singing along with "Tears of a Clown." We're good. We just need to get rid of the bleach bottle and get back to the cottage.

Fuck, somebody's coming. I hear heavy footsteps on the ground, coming fast from somewhere. Steve darts into the darkness, back toward the creek. We should split up. I go the other way.

I run across the yard, along the property line, toward the old apple tree. Ow, fuck. I fall. I think I stepped in a hole. I heard something pop in my ankle. Feels like 188 degrees in there all of a sudden.

I try and get up and run again, but my ankle collapses. Somebody is coming. This is not good. I can hear the footsteps. I'm afraid to look up and I can't run on my ankle how it is.

Steve is gone in the darkness. I try and get up again, but I can't put any weight on my ankle at all. It crumbles underneath me again. I lie facedown in the wet grass and try and crawl away.

Whoever is behind me is getting closer. Oh fuck, I hope it's not Mr. Richardson. I don't want to get fucking arrested.

I roll over and look at the person standing over me. He's backlit by the headlights from the party, but I can tell who it is by the silhouette. It's the fucking Sinister Minister. Oh shit. That's even worse than getting caught by the cops.

He's probably going to take me hostage and put me in the back of his white van and kidnap me. Or just flat out murder me right here.

He's just looking down at me. He isn't saying anything. His white hair is blowing up into the air and he almost looks like an angel from that movie about angels with Nicolas Cage in his black trench coat.

He reaches his hand out to me, like he wants to help me up, but the only problem with that is I fucking hate the guy. I don't want to touch his creepy, pasty-white Christian Confederate hand. Fuck that.

I shake my head a little. I'll just lie here until my parents see me out here, or Steve tells them I'm here, or something. I'll just lie here until someone comes and saves me.

The minister hasn't moved his hand. He's just holding it out there, waiting for me to take it. I don't want to take it. I don't want to give him the satisfaction of having held his hand out there long enough for me to take it.

I keep waiting for my parents to come rushing over here and save me, but it's been a few minutes now and I don't think they're going to. I just don't think they're going to.

Oh fuck it. I reach up and take his hand and he pulls me to my feet in one motion. I can't put any weight on my ankle, but I think I've got good enough balance to hop my way back to the cottage.

I say, "Thanks," and hop over to the apple tree a few feet away.

He doesn't say anything. He just stands there backlit by the headlights, and then once he sees that I can get from one tree to another, he turns around and goes back into his cottage.

I hop back into the cottage without anyone seeing me. I can't find Steve anywhere. I wonder if he got caught on the way back.

I go into the bedroom. He's in bed already. What the fuck?

I say, "Dude, you totally abandoned me."

"Fuck, did you get nabbed?"

"No. Kind of. The minister saw me."

"What did he say? Is he going to tell your parents? Am I going to have to go home on a bus or something?"

"No, dude, he's not going to talk to my parents. He's not as bad as he seems."

"Really?"

I don't know why I said that. I'm not sure why I think that. I stand, leaning against the wall, on one foot. What else is there to say?

I say, "So are you going to bed, or what?"

"Yeah, aren't you?"

"I don't know if I can sleep. My ankle is killing me."

"Oh well, dude, at least we didn't get caught."

"Yeah, I guess."

I'm sitting at the picnic table looking at the sunrise while everyone else is still sleeping. I couldn't sleep because my ankle was hurting so much. It isn't broken, I don't think, because I can put a little bit of weight on it. It feels like it did when I sprained it in soccer. I put some ice on it and it's resting on the bench and it's feeling better.

I lie back on the bench and watch the sun oranging up the black sky. I feel peaceful for the first time this summer. Maybe I should sleep out on the picnic table for the rest of the time here.

Mom wakes up first and comes outside in her purple bathrobe with a cup of coffee in her hand. I almost never see her in the morning before she's had a cup of coffee, especially the morning after she's gotten all drunk with her friends. I don't know what time they all left, but it had to be after midnight.

She sits down next to me at the picnic table, and I have to sit up so the table doesn't flip over on top of us. That would be a great *America's Funniest Home Videos* moment.

She takes a sip of her coffee and rubs between my shoulders with her other hand. She must have done that when I was a baby, because it always makes me feel weirdly sleepy.

She whispers, "Good morning," as quietly as she can, and I can't tell if she's whispering to not ruin the serenity or if she's whispering because she has a massive hangover.

I don't say anything. I feel like asking "How drunk did you get last night?" but I don't. I'm not mad, but it was a little disgusting what she and her friends were doing. I hate it when they act like teenagers.

Steve and I are the teenagers. We're the ones who are supposed to do stupid shit and then be hung over the next morning. I feel like going back to bed. Maybe I can get some sleep now.

"I'm going back to bed."

I get up and start hopping across the lawn on my one good foot, but Mom notices and switches into Mom mode. She's not whispering anymore. "Whoa, whoa, whoa. What is happening with your ankle?"

I look down at it. It's not very pretty. Purple and swollen to twice the size of the other one. "Uh, I don't know. Good night."

"Wait. Come back here. Let me look at that thing."

"Why? It's fine. It's just swollen."

"It's not just swollen. It's bruised too. What happened?"

"Nothing." I start hopping away again, but she comes over to me.

"I'm not letting you go back to bed with your ankle like that." Mom studied nursing for a while in college, so she thinks that she can diagnose things. Usually, I don't care, but now I just want to get back to bed.

"Mom, are you a doctor?"

"No, but—"

"Are you a nurse?"

"No, I'm not—"

"Then let me go back to bed."

I turn around and start hopping away again on my one good ankle. I expect her to start after me or say something, but she doesn't. She just lets me hop across the lawn.

I'm about to get to the screen door, but with all this hopping, my ankle is really hurting now. I get to the screen door, and just as I'm about to open it, I glance back at her one more time.

She's just looking at me. It's like she can tell how much it hurts and is just waiting for me to ask for help. The shitty thing is that it really does hurt. I don't know what to do.

I look at her and I don't say anything, but she can tell by the look on my face that I've given up.

We're on our way to the emergency room, and my foot is up on the dashboard. Fuck, the bottom of my foot is really dirty from walking around with no shoes on. I wish I had time to wash it. This is going to be embarrassing.

I'm staring out the window watching the Sunday-morning sunshine spread over the hills. I used to think this place was beautiful, but I don't know why I thought that. It's just a really crappy area. It's so cheap-looking. Look at that barn. It's totally collapsing and no one is doing anything about it. That's why we can afford to come here every summer, because this is like the ghetto. We have a cottage in the ghetto. Well, the rural ghetto. What's that called—the boonies?

I don't care. It's terrible. It's such shit. There's not even anything to do around here. It's just swimming and waiting for time to pass. I don't know what I ever saw in this place. I really don't. It's just a fucking crapper.

Mom is listening to NPR and humming along with the theme song from the show. I wonder why you get so boring when you get old. Look at her. She's a mom and she's a wife, but she doesn't have a passion for anything. She doesn't have any real reason to live.

What is she doing in the world that's making it better? She's driving her son to the emergency room. Whoop-de-fucking-do.

"Mom," I say, "what did you want to be when you were a little girl? When you grew up, I mean."

She glances over at me and gives me one of those looks like she's expecting me to attack her. Do I attack her? Was I going to attack her? I don't know. Maybe I was going to, but now I sort of feel sorry for her. "Why do you ask?"

"Just curious." I try and make my voice sound a little less threatening than it did the first time.

"You really want to know?"

"Yeah. Why, is it like a big secret or something?"

"No. It's just you never asked me anything like that before."

"So, I'm asking now."

She looks at me sideways. She's still a little tentative. "When I was a little girl, I actually really wanted to be a doctor."

"Really?"

"Yup, I wanted to study medicine. I had this big old anatomy book I took from my parents' bookshelf that was filled with these amazing color drawings of the human body. And I used to sit up in my room and go through the whole book, page by page. I used to pick an artery in one of the pictures and follow it all the way through the body."

"Wow." That's weird. I've never imagined my mom being a little girl before. I mean, I've seen pictures of her, but I've never actually imagined what she was like when she was little. Now, in my head, I've got this picture of her dreaming of being a doctor. "So why didn't you become a doctor? Not smart enough?"

She smiles. I think she knows that was a joke. "No, I met Dad, and we decided to get married. And then I put my career on hold for a while, while he got his business started, and then we had you."

"Oh, so do you like hate me or something because I ruined your dreams of becoming a doctor?"

"You're joking, right?"

"No. Not really."

"No. I don't hate you. I love being your mom, and I wouldn't give that up for anything in the world."

"That's corny." She doesn't say anything after that. Whoops, maybe I was just an asshole, but she was being corny. It was like an after-school special in here all of a sudden.

The emergency room is filled with people. I thought it would be empty except for us on Sunday morning. I thought everyone would be in bed or in church.

There are at least three people here with bloody hands wrapped up in dish towels. I whisper, "Mom, why do you think there are so many people here with cuts? Do you think there was like a knife fight or something?"

She looks around like it's the first time she's noticed anyone else is even here. "I'm not sure. It might be bagels."

"Bagels?"

"Accidents with cutting bagels. I think there are a lot of those on Sunday mornings."

"Hmm." I didn't know that.

One of the women behind a counter calls my name, and they wheel me back into a room.

I hope my ankle isn't broken or something. That would suck for soccer. The doctor comes in and asks a bunch of questions, touches my ankle, which really hurts, and then sends me back out to get an X-ray.

They push me back into the room and I lie down on the butcher paper. I'm so tired. Even with these bright white lights staring down at me, I feel like I could go to sleep.

Finally, the doctor comes back in and tells me that it's not broken, it's just a really bad sprain. I've got to keep the weight off of it for three weeks, so I get crutches and a brace to keep my ankle from moving.

Shit.

We're driving home with my foot in the boot. We picked up a prescription for pain medicine at the drugstore, and I took some. At least now the throbbing in my ankle has gone away, but the inside of my head feels like it's been lined with cotton balls and I can't really hear. Actually, I can hear everything they're saying on NPR, but I can't figure out what they're talking about anymore.

138

I still hear the words, but it's like they have to get translated back from English into English for me to understand them. I don't have the energy to do that right now.

I look out the window at the landscape rushing by. I like looking at one spot in the distance, like that tree in the middle of that field, and then watching how the rest of the landscape moves in relation to it. The things up close move so much faster than the things in the distance. Now I'm feeling carsick. I close my eyes.

Mom turns down our driveway and I open my eyes. It's still pretty early. I wonder if anyone is up yet. We park under the old pine and Mom helps me out of the car. I crutch over to the picnic table and sit down. My foot is throbbing, so I put it up on the bench.

No one seems to be up yet, except the Richardsons' car is gone, so they're probably at church. Mom went inside to do some stuff. I'm happy to just sit here and look at the lake. I'm glad everyone is still sleeping. I'm sick of everybody.

Steve and I are playing cards at the picnic table and watching Mr. Richardson mow his lawn just like he does every Sunday. God, I feel like I've watched him do this a million times. I guess I used to feel like it was funny to watch him walking up and down his lawn in these precise lines, with his shirt off and his enormous, hairy man boobs jiggling and swinging like pendulums along the way. I used to think it was kind of interesting to compare his back hair to his chest hair. I thought it was amazing how much he looks like one of those silverback gorillas. I never noticed how he wants everything in his life to be perfect and how he spends all his

139

time mowing his lawn and weeding his yard and working but never seems to enjoy any of it.

He hasn't seen the cross yet, but I can see it from here. It came out pretty well. The grass all died overnight and turned this nasty brown color. It looks like a cross, except the top is a little sloppy where Steve rushed it. I can't believe Mr. Richardson hasn't seen it yet. He will in about thirty-seven seconds.

He sees it. He turns off the lawn mower and walks over to the patch of dead grass shaped like a cross in his lawn. On the TV show, the guy started screaming and yelling, and it was hilarious because he was on TV, but that's not what Mr. Richardson is doing.

Mr. Richardson is standing, looking at the cross. His body is still. The only thing that's moving is the hair on his back.

He just stands there for a long time and then he turns around, walks to his garage, and comes back with a shovel. He wedges the shovel into the grass and starts digging it up.

Wow, no screaming or yelling. No emotion at all. I guess either he's not mad or he's holding it all inside. That's disappointing. I wanted to see him freak out.

Steve and I look at each other. I raise my eyebrows and he shrugs.

I get up from the picnic table. I say, "I'm going to take a shower." The soccer ball is in my way, so I hit it with my crutch in the direction of the Richardsons' cottage. I watch it roll right to the property line, where the beautiful, perfect lawn meets the crappy lawn, and crutch all the way back into the cottage.

Steve follows me in and we sit down on the green

vinyl couch and look out the window. Mr. Richardson has stopped digging up the grass cross and walked over to the soccer ball. He gives it a little kick, just to get it off of his lawn.

Steve and I were going to go up to the waterfall, but I can't make it with my ankle how it is. So we're just sitting at the picnic table shooting the shit and hoping that Sophie walks by in her bikini.

Kay and Roger and Claire pull up in their Volvo. I guess they wanted to hang out one last time before we have to go back home. The adults all go down to the water and Claire sits down at the picnic table with us. She's wearing a wide-brimmed hat like an old lady.

She says, "How's your ankle?"

"It's feeling better." Why does she even bother asking? She knows we hate each other.

Steve says, "Hi, I'm Steve."

"I'm Claire."

"Hey, it's really nice to meet you, Claire." He reaches out and shakes her hand. What's up with that? Did I forget to tell him that Claire and I hate each other?

Steve has a way of acting all sweet and nice around girls, but somehow they still know that he wants to hook up with them. Whenever I act nice around girls, they always think I want to be their brother or their best friend.

Steve says, "So how long have you known this joker?" pointing at me.

"Way too long." Claire laughs and Steve laughs too. They're doing that thing where the only thing they have in

141

common is they both know me, so the only thing they can do is make fun of me.

Steve says, "So tell me something about our mutual friend here." He points to me again. Stop pointing at me, Steve.

"You want to hear a story about Luke?"

"Yes I do."

I'm not going to just sit here and let them embarrass me. I say, "Claire, tell about the time you told on me for crossing the street in front of your house. Or the time you told on me for saying 'Shut up' in your yard. Tell about that."

Claire shrugs it off. "Well, one time, I had to spend the afternoon over at Luke's house because my parents were doing I don't know what, taking our dog to the vet or something. Luke and I lived only a few houses away from each other, but I hated going over to his house because, well, you know."

Steve says, "It kind of smells weird, right?"

"You noticed that too!"

I say, "That's not my fault. That's the curry chicken my mom always makes."

"So anyway, I went over to his house, and he was in his bedroom, and you have to remember we were like six at the time. . . ."

"Yeah, go on." Is he really into this story or is he just flirting with her?

"He had taken everything in his room—like everything, the toys, all the clothes out of the drawers, books—and he'd thrown it all on the floor. I came in and he was standing on top of his bed, with this really crazy look on his face and just a pair of underwear on, and he yelled, 'Careful! It's a flood!'"

Steve is laughing, but I don't understand. What's so funny about that? A lot of kids make their rooms into disaster areas.

"And he made me stand on the bed with him and pretend we were in a flood. And when his mom found us in there, she got mad at me for not telling her what was going on."

Steve punches me in the shoulder and says, "Dude, you were such a little asshole."

"Yeah." I punch him back. I don't know why I thought it would be fun having him here.

We're going home tomorrow and I'm glad. I've never felt like this before, but I'm just kind of sick of the whole scene this year. I'm sick of my parents and their friends and Steve and the Richardsons and the minister and the Vizquels. They're all so stupid. I don't even know if I want to come back next year.

I sit down in the chair next to the old brown phone and put my foot up on one of the kitchen chairs. I don't know how I'm going to get in shape for soccer practice with my ankle like this. Hopefully, the brace will help and I'll be able to get my feet under me again. Soccer practice starts in about a week. I hope I can at least get on the JV team, and maybe even varsity if I'm lucky.

Steve and I are sitting in the car waiting for Mom and Dad to say good-bye to the lake. I wish they would hurry up so we can get on the road. I can't wait to get back home and watch some TV and play some video games.

Steve is sitting in the front seat for now, playing with the radio. My leg is up, but it still hurts. I want to get out of here. I say, "Honk the horn."

Steve looks back at me to see if I'm joking. I'm not, so he does, and Mom and Dad both turn around and give us the evil eye. I guess that ruined their little romantic moment by the lake. I don't care. I want to get the fuck out of here.

They're walking back to the car, but they both look pissed. Steve gets out and gets in the back with me. No one says anything as they get in the car, but it's the kind of not saying something that means we're not talking.

Dad forces out, "Good-bye, lake," as he throws the car into reverse and pulls fast out of the parking area. The car bumps a little. We must have run over something. Dad gets out and pulls the flattened soccer ball from under the tire.

"Goddamnit, Luke."

16

Ever since I got my learner's permit, I've been realizing what a bad driver Dad is. Mom's sitting in the back because her legs are so much shorter than mine now, and I've got my headphones on, listening to Rage Against the Machine, to take my mind off it, but it's not working. The way Dad is driving is really pissing me off. The way he puts his foot on the gas and pumps it a little, just to get his speed up to fifty-five, and then takes his foot off the gas as soon as he gets there. Then when the car drops down to like forty-eight, he gives it just enough gas to make the needle kiss fifty-five again. If he really wants to be stuck at fifty-five, why doesn't he just put on the fucking cruise control? I mean seriously, I'm getting carsick.

We take the turn down toward the lake, and I get that feeling in my stomach I used to get when I was little, or maybe I'm just hungover. The lake is still here.

We drive past all the old landmarks. They tore down that old barn that was sinking into the earth, and it looks like they're building a house where it used to be. They repainted the Wirth mansion, but they used this really ugly light green paint on the trim. It looks terrible. The house shaped like a tepee used to have a nice yard, but now it's overgrown and disgusting. The dairy farm that got turned into a winery is looking all fancy and new. They turned the old tractor barn into a little restaurant.

Everything changes, I guess. That's not really a surprise, but I still don't like it. We pull into the driveway, and the old, dying pine scrapes the roof of the car. The Vizquels are still here. The minister's red-cross van is parked in front of his cottage, and Mr. Richardson is out working on his lawn.

Maybe nothing changes. Maybe everything *seems* to change but actually never does. I turn off the Rage and say, "Mom, do you know where my bathing suit is?"

"It's in the black suitcase under the white T-shirts."

I knew that, but I kind of wanted to hear her say it anyway.

I miss Jennifer already. I want to call her, but I don't want to talk to her in front of Mom and Dad. God, I miss everything about her.

I'm not sure why I'm even here. I mean, I'm not a kid anymore. I don't really like fishing or jumping off the docks. I just wish Jennifer could have come with us. I don't see what the big deal is. Her parents were fine with it. It's only Mom who thinks it would be inappropriate for Jennifer and me to sleep together.

I told her we would sleep in a tent in the front yard, but that didn't make a difference. I mean, what would be the problem?

This isn't the eighteenth century. People sleep together

before they get married. Mom and Dad slept together before they got married. So why can't Jennifer and I sleep together before we get married?

Anyway, I just wish she were here. We could go out in the canoe and make out. We could go skinny-dipping and sleep on the dock. We could buy our own food and cook it. We could take the car out and make out.

We walk down to the beach, past the woodpile and a giant pile of rocks, some as big as bowling balls. There's the beginnings of a stone wall along the Richardsons' property line. I guess Mr. Richardson has finally had enough of those dogs. Dad says, "A wall." And leaves it at that.

I'm still wearing shoes. There's a layer of plastic between me and the earth. I don't like it. I strip off my shoes and socks and tiptoe across the rocks to the edge of the lake. The water is like a mirror, but it's reflecting all the wrong stuff.

Mom and Dad are standing behind me. It's our first night back and the only thing they're talking about is the minister and how they can't believe that he still has the Confederate flag up. I can hear the dogs barking inside his house.

I never thought I'd say this, but I'm almost happy to see that the minister still has his flag up. It's just kind of funny to see how everybody reacts to it. My parents are so liberal and are all about free speech and the First Amendment, but only when it doesn't involve a Confederate flag.

The Richardsons are out on their dock, and Mom walks over to talk to them about it. She is really letting this whole thing get to her.

I walk over and say hi to the Richardsons too. They barely acknowledge me. All they want to talk about is the minister. I guess the breaking news is that he has a woman who sleeps there sometimes and they're not married. Scandalous. And apparently, she has a little daughter from some other relationship. God, I wish Jennifer were here.

Live and let live, that's what Jennifer would say. One of the things I really love about Jennifer is that she always has a good perspective on life. A positive attitude. She always says if you go through life with a negative attitude, things are going to be so much harder than they would be if you just looked on the bright side.

I walk down to the beach and check my cell phone to see if there's any messages from her, but I'm getting almost no service up here. That fucking sucks. Now I wish I hadn't come up this year at all. I could have stayed at Steve's. This is going to be the worst two weeks of my life.

I'm going out on the Richardsons' dock to get some sun. They're letting us use it so we can get a little farther away from the minister and the dogs. The boards on the dock are hot, so I lay my towel over them and lie down on my stomach. I'm so glad to be away from everyone. I just want to lie in the sun and think about Jennifer.

Last winter, Jennifer and I were lying up in her bed together, not even doing anything sexual, just keeping each other warm, and she had this old Lava lamp that she'd gotten for Christmas, and she turned it on and we just lay there staring at it and holding each other.

We kept asking each other what we were thinking about, staring at the red globs floating in the yellow fluid, and Jennifer was always thinking about something different, either poetry or a book that she was reading. I told her I was thinking about music or trying to define the word "art." But I never told her what I was really thinking about.

I was thinking about those famous photographs of a baby in the womb and how the red globs in the Lava lamp looked just like that baby developing. And then I thought about how much I wanted to have a baby with Jennifer.

I know we're not old enough yet, but later, when we get married after college, we're going to have a baby together and raise it to be really open-minded and to have all sorts of passions for music and art and cinema.

Anyway, that's what I used to think about before we had the pregnancy scare in the spring and I stopped thinking about that.

She's at theater camp right now. I'm going to write her a letter, just so she knows I'm thinking about her. I get up off the dock and walk right through the Richardsons' yard. I walk into the cottage and tear a few pieces of paper off the pad next to the telephone.

I look up at the painting that's above the green couch. I don't know why, but I've never really looked at it before. It's an oil painting of waves breaking over rocks. Where did we get that? Has it been here the whole time?

Whatever, I'm just going to write what I feel.

Dear Jennifer,
How are you? I miss you. I hope you know that. I think about you all the time (not like that). Well, actually, like that.
So I'm just up here without you. I still hope you can come up here next summer so I can show you all the pieces of my childhood that I've talked so

much about. I want you to know me better than anyone. You already do, but you know what I mean. Completely.

It's only seventeen days until I see you again. That's 408 hours—24,480 minutes. I figured that out myself, without a calendar, so I deserve a little credit. Don't you think?

I actually meant to write "calculator," but my words are escaping me. I need you to be here with me to remind me when I use the wrong word or phrase or something in the wrong way. I love it when you correct my grammar.

Anyway, that's all for now. I'll write you again soon. Hope you're having fun at theater camp. Don't make out with any hot guys—or girls, for that matter. You're the only one for me. I love you. Completely.

Love,

Luke

That's awesome. That's an awesome letter. I know she's going to love it. I hope Mom has stamps. I'm going to put it in the mailbox.

Mike and Eliza are down for the weekend and their daughter, Emma, is wobbling around on the lawn like a spinning top. I try not to have too much to do with Mike and Eliza because they're kind of crazy. I remember that time I was hanging out over there and Eliza got all weird.

I'm not sure what to make of that, but I just remember it was kind of a weird situation. It reminds me of the Seamus

Heaney poem that Jennifer loves, about how he's a writer, and his dad and granddad were diggers, but he can't dig like they used to, so he just digs with his pen.

I like that poem, but I can't remember what it has to do with Mike and Eliza. Nothing probably. I just miss Jennifer.

Got a letter in the mail from Jennifer. I'm so excited. God, it even smells like her.

> Sweet Luke,
>
> Wanted to write and explain why I haven't—written, that is. So busy. So so so busy. But it's amazing here. The instructors are brilliant. YOU would love it. You should have come. Ah well.
>
> Mom and Dad came and visited and asked about you, which is embarrassing because that means they actually do love you more than me. Not joking.
>
> Sooooo, what have you been doing? Lake stuff? Sounds like fun—kind of. I mean, it does sound like fun, but I wish you were here. You would LOVE it.
>
> I'm sending a photo so you can meet some of my sweet mates (just kidding—suite). From the left it's Angela, Christina, Chelsea, and Robin. And me, of course—you remember me, right?
>
> LOVE without borders,
> Jenn
> P.S. If you call here at eight o'clock on

Tuesday night, someone you love might just be waiting by the phone.

P.P.S. I wrote you a poem.

Silent rivers run
underground no one knows where
like my lust for you.

That's sweet. God, I miss her.

I look at the picture. The girls are all smiling for the camera in the cheesiest way possible and doing jazz hands in a dance studio. They all look like really nice girls and a lot of them are really hot.

In the background of the photo there's a big mirror and I can see the flash of the camera reflected in the mirror. I can also see the person who's taking the picture. It's a guy. He looks tall and he has messy brown hair.

I don't recognize him, but that doesn't mean anything, because there's no reason that I should recognize him. He's probably a teacher or maybe one of the other girls' boyfriends. I'll have to ask Jenn about him when I talk to her on Tuesday.

I've been watching Mr. Richardson work on his stone wall while I pretend to read my Stephen King book. Shirtless in the sun, his hair wet and matted to his chest and back—that's the way he likes it.

He brings the wheelbarrow over to the mountain of rocks and loads up about ten of the bowling balls. They're heavy obviously, because his old-man arms shake as he lifts them up and into the wheelbarrow. Then he brings them over to his work area and lays them all out on the grass. He looks at them for a while like he's figuring out how to put a jigsaw puzzle together and then he stacks them into his wall. He's not using mortar or anything, so it's pretty amazing that the wall is holding up at all. I know it wouldn't if I were building it. I bet he thinks I'm lazy just sitting here and watching him work, but I'm not lazy. I actually don't feel like helping him.

I walk over, sort of in his direction and sort of in the direction of the water. I haven't decided if I'm going to say anything to him.

I get within ten feet and he says, "Cool Hand Luke," just like he used to, but he doesn't look up.

I say, "Hey, Mr. Richardson, whatcha workin' on?"

"A wall."

"Yeah, how's that going?" He's finished about ten feet, and he's got about another hundred and fifty to go.

"It's going." I knew he was going to say that. I look over at the big rock pile, and I almost offer to help him wheel a few loads over, but I don't, because I hate that he's building this thing. I really hate it.

"Well, keep up the good work." I'm not sure if he can tell that I don't mean it.

"Will do."

I walk down to the lake and skip a stone. The feeling doesn't go away.

I got a postcard from Jennifer. She must have gotten my letter. It's on the back of one of those free postcards you can get from a restaurant. It has a picture of a bunch of daisies blooming and a few cows chomping on them in a field. There's a poem written on the back.

Distance is a bitch
A flower eaten by cows
Our love becomes shit

I love her sense of humor. It's brilliant. The cows eating the daisies and all that. It's just a little depressing to read that last line, "Our love becomes shit." I'm going to call her tonight at eight.

It's seven-fifty. I check my cell phone. No service. I pick up the house phone to call Jennifer, but someone is on the fucking party line. I can't make a call until they hang up. This sucks.

I hang up the phone and sit down on the green couch and stare at the phone. I wonder who's on the phone. It's probably the minister.

I look out the window across the lawn. Yup, he's on the phone. Pacing back and forth, wrapping the cord around his hand like a twelve-year-old girl.

I pick up the phone lightly and listen without breathing.

"Hey, what are you watching?"

A thin voice on the other end of the line says, "*Matlock.*"

"Oh yeah? You having fun?"

I can't tell if the voice is a really old woman or a little girl. The voice is strange. I think it might be a little girl, because I can hardly understand her, but it could be an old woman who had a stroke.

He says, "You can watch that when you get here. What did you have for dinner?"

"Hot dogs."

"Were they good?"

"Yeah."

"Ha-ha."

Oh for fuck's sake. I can't believe he's talking about hot dogs. I say, "Excuse me, I need to use the phone."

He pauses for a second and then says, "So what did you have on the hot dogs?"

"Mustard and relish."

"Yeah? That sounds good."

I try and say it with more force. "Excuse me, I need to use the phone."

He doesn't even pause this time. He just continues his stupid conversation.

He's ignoring me. What a dickhead.

I walk out of the house and stare straight at him. He's not looking over here. I walk out into the middle of the lawn and stare at him. He is the biggest asshole in the world. I can't believe I ever thought he wasn't. He still won't look at me.

This is bullshit. All right, I'm not going to get caught up in this bullshit just like everybody else. I'm going to calm down. I walk down to the lake. I walk past him, but I don't look at him.

He says, "So did you have any ketchup?"

He's got to be talking to a little kid. I try and skip a stone. I get a couple, but nothing spectacular.

The summer light is fading and the moon is rising up over the lake, and it looks like an orange lollipop. I should write a poem about that for Jennifer.

> Moon like a lollipop,
> Orange or mustard-colored.
> What did you have for dinner?
> Hot dogs? That sounds good.

Fuck it. It's almost eight o'clock and I need to use the phone. I stomp back toward the minister's house. He's gone inside, but he's still talking on the phone. I can hear him through the sliding screen door. The dogs are growling, but at least they're inside the house.

"Yeah, should I put mustard on mine?"

I say, "Excuse me, I need to use the phone."

He looks up like he can't believe I have the guts to talk to him. He says, "Hold on," into the phone and then looks back at me. "What do you want?"

"I need the phone. It's important."

"I'm using it. You can use it when I'm done."

"No, you don't understand. I can only call right now. This is when I can call. I need to use the phone."

The minister turns his back to me and says, "Hey, sorry about that. What were you saying? Oh yeah, what kind of mustard should I put on it?"

I can't believe this fucking guy. I would hit him, but he probably outweighs me by a hundred pounds. Fuck.

I walk back down to the beach and sit in the plastic chair. Shit, now what do I do? My fucking cell phone doesn't work around here, and I have no idea where the nearest pay phone is. I guess I could just wait and use the phone when he's done, but who knows when that's going to fucking be? I wish I could use the phone just for a minute. Just so I can tell her I love her.

I look around. The Richardsons are on the same party line, and so are the Vizquels.

This is bullshit. I just want to call my girlfriend. Why doesn't my stupid fucking cell phone work here? Try it again. Jesus, there's not even one little bar on the thing. Fuck, I wish I had my license and a car.

I start walking up the driveway to the road, watching the screen on my phone. I have to find a place that has cell phone reception. As soon as my feet hit the pavement, I start sprinting. I'm not in soccer shape yet, so I can only sprint as far as the four-way stop sign where the broken-down old gas station is. There's no pay phone here, and my phone is still fucking useless.

Now which way? I've got to pick a direction. Up the hill. That's probably the best for cell phone reception. If I had been thinking when I left, I would have brought my bike, but I wasn't thinking. I could go back, but I don't like to do that.

I've got this weird thing about going back the same way I came. I just hate to do it. It feels unnatural to me, like there's a blockade behind me. Whenever possible, I go in a loop to get back to where I came from.

I jog up the hill, past the house where they breed the scary dogs. One of them starts barking at me and it's so loud it actually hurts my ears and makes the hair on my neck stand up.

I hope that thing is on a leash. I'm sure he's on a leash. He's on a leash, right? Fuck, he's chasing me. I hear someone with a Canadian accent call out, "Klaus, come here!"

I run again as fast as I can, and I can hear the dog getting closer. I keep running and I hear the Canadian guy call out again, and this time the dog stops chasing. I keep running. I'm not going to stop running until I put some distance between me and the fucking dog. I get as far as the Civil War graveyard and run in and hide in back of the iron fence, among all the little gravestones. I can't catch my breath.

I lie down. I still can't breathe. I check my phone. Nothing. When I was younger, we used to come up here every once in a while. We'd park at the modern graveyard right next door and then walk through here and down the old path to the waterfall.

This little graveyard used to be all covered with weeds and bushes and vines and crap until, I don't know what happened, but they cleaned it all up.

Each one of these guys just has the smallest little piece of stone with his name on it, the day he was born, and the day he died. Some of them are so worn away by time and acid rain that I can't even read them.

Next door at the modern graveyard, there's a whole mess of people with huge monuments to themselves. They all have quotes from famous poets and long lists of family members, but when you really think about it, the Civil War guys had it right. Maybe it all just comes down to the day you were born and the day you died. That's all that's left.

Nobody writes on their gravestone HAD A REALLY GOOD SANDWICH—MAY 17, 1987. Or FINALLY GOT CELL PHONE SERVICE—JULY 15, 2008. It's just birth and death. Birth and death.

I've got to get out of here. This is too depressing. I walk out of the graveyard and back onto the road. I'm just going to keep walking up the hill until I get at least two bars on my stupid cell phone. I don't care how far I have to go.

I get all the way to the big cornfield before I get service. I pull the piece of paper out of my pocket and dial the number. Come on. Come on. It's ringing. Yes. Answer the phone. It's still ringing. Answer the phone.

"Hello."

"Jennifer?"

"No. This is Megan. Who's this?"

"I'm a friend of Jennifer's. I was supposed to call her at eight, but I didn't get a chance to. Is she there? Is she around?"

"You know what, I think she went out."

"What time is it?"

"It's like eight-twenty. So yeah, she's not here. Do you want me to like take a message or something?"

"Yeah, yeah, thanks, just let her know that I called and I'm really sorry that it took so long but I'll explain everything."

"Okay, you want me to write that down?"

"No, I guess not. Just tell her I called."

"Yeah, but who are you? What's your name?"

"Luke. I'm her boyfriend."

"All right. I'll tell her when they get back. Bye."

"Wait, when who gets back? Who is she out with?" Shit, she's gone. She hung up. Fuck. What did she mean, "when they get back"? Did she mean like a group of people? Like a whole bunch of people? Or did she mean Jennifer and one other person?

We don't have very good pronouns in English. There should be a pronoun for when it's two people doing something, compared to a whole group of people. One person is easy: she did it or he did it. But when it's two or eight, it's the same: They are out. They aren't coming back.

It's not that I'm jealous, because I know that Jennifer would never, ever do anything with anyone else, but it still kind of bothers me. Fuck, I just wish I could talk to her. I just really need to get ahold of her. Come on.

What did that fucking girl mean, "when they get back"?

When *they* get back. Where did they go? What were they doing? I guess, what *are* they doing, because they're doing it right now. I don't want to even think it, but I can't help it. Is she screwing another guy? She wouldn't do that, would she? Would she?

I don't think so. Right? She's just not that kind of girl. Except who was that guy taking the picture, that tall guy with the messy brown hair? I don't want to be thinking this, but I can just imagine . . . I can just imagine the kind of thing that's going on.

Whatever happens. Whatever happens, I'm always going to love you, Jennifer. I'm always going to love you.

I walk back to the cottage, past the Vizquels' house and the minister's cottage. His van is gone. At least now I can use the phone. Jennifer should be back by now.

Mom and Dad are reading on the couch. They both have their reading glasses on. They look really old.

"Hey, Luke, where were you?"

"Trying to get cell phone service."

"Any luck?"

"Not really."

I walk over and pick up the phone. There's no dial tone. There's only a fast busy signal. It sounds like an ambulance in England. "If you'd like to make a call, please hang up and try again."

I hang up. That's weird. I pick up the phone again. "If you'd like to make a call, please hang up and try again."

I hang up again. What's happening? What is the deal? The minister isn't home. Why does the phone sound like it's off the hook?

Oh shit, I think I know what's happening. The minister left his phone off the hook. I go outside and look across at his cottage. All the lights are off except one, but that doesn't mean the phone isn't off the hook. I walk across the lawn and head toward the minister's cottage.

I don't see anyone in the cottage. I just see the light on, but it's not enough light for a person to be in there. It's a light you leave on when you leave and you don't want anyone to know you've gone. There's no one home. I don't think there is anyway. I want to make sure, though, so he doesn't come out with a shotgun and kill me. The dogs aren't barking. He must have taken them with him.

I realize I've been walking on my tiptoes to keep from making noise. I walk up to the sliding glass doors and try and look in to see if anyone is in there. I don't see anything except for one little bare lightbulb hanging over the sink. It looks really weird in there.

I can't just be peeking in the window, though. What if someone is home? I have to knock. Fuck, I don't want to do this, but I just really need to call Jennifer. I just really have to talk to her.

I knock three times on the glass door, and it sounds hollow, like there's nothing at all inside the house.

I can't tell if anyone is coming, because it's so dark in there, so I knock again, this time louder, so the whole neighborhood can hear it.

Jesus, how did I get myself into this situation? I see another light come on inside. Oh great, he's home. Okay. I'll just say, "Hi, I'm sorry, but your phone is off the hook."

I can't really see him at all through the door, but I can tell there's a shape moving toward me in the darkness. He

163

doesn't look as big as he did earlier, which is just bizarre. Maybe it's the girlfriend.

The door opens and there's a little girl standing in front of me. She's maybe six years old, and I've never seen her before. She's kind of cute. She's got these big brown eyes that look sad, like a cartoon of a hound dog. She's wearing a little white nightgown. She looks like she was sleeping, but it's not that late, is it? Maybe for a kid.

I say, "Hi, I'm your neighbor. Is your mommy or daddy home?"

She looks up at me like I'm made out of clear plastic and she's looking at the trees and sky behind me. She doesn't say anything, or shake her head, or give any indication that I'm really even here. The way she's acting, it almost makes me wonder if I'm dreaming. Am I dreaming?

The little girl turns her back to me and walks away back down the hall and goes into a room. She left the door open, though, so I'm not sure if she's going to get the minister or if she's just going back to bed. This is weird. Maybe I'm supposed to go inside. I don't know what to do. I step inside.

I look around. This isn't at all what I expected. There are piss-soaked newspapers on the floor and clothes folded neatly on all the furniture, like someone is about to move. There's nowhere to sit down. There's a skillet on the stove with what looks like what used to be onions or peppers in it, but they're so overcooked it could be anything. There's a window open somewhere, and the drapes look like they're breathing.

I just got the creeps. I got that feeling that someone is watching me and that I'm not supposed to be here, but if someone didn't want me to be here, why wouldn't they just tell me that? What would be the point of hiding?

I walk a little farther into the cottage. What am I doing? I shouldn't be doing this. But I really have to find a way to call Jennifer. She's probably back from being out and waiting by the phone.

Where is that white phone with the thirty-foot cord? I don't see it anywhere. Wait, there it is, all the way across the room, sitting on top of a pile of clothes.

I walk like an Indian across the floor. I just have to hang up the phone, and then I'll get out of here. This is too freaky. The smell in here is disgusting. It's like rotten apples, paint thinner, and dog piss.

I hope nobody comes around the corner and sees me standing in the middle of the living room. That would be kind of difficult to explain. Finally, I get to the receiver and pick it up. I follow the cord over to the phone on the kitchen wall and hang it up.

Should I just call from here? I don't want to talk on the phone while my parents are listening. I'll just call from here and get it over with.

I pull the number out of my pocket and dial. It's ringing. Holy shit. I shouldn't be in here. I'm just about ready to pass out. It's like ten o'clock. I hope she's there. Jesus, I hope she's back from wherever they went.

"Hello." Someone answers the phone, but it's not her.

"Oh, hi, is, um, Jennifer there?"

"Jennifer?"

"Yeah, Jennifer O'Neil."

"Does she have brown hair?"

"Well, kind of, uh, I guess it's maybe dirty blond."

"Oh, okay. I think she's kind of busy."

Busy, really? What could she be doing? "Well, can you tell her that her boyfriend is on the phone?"

"Hold on." She puts down the phone and starts talking to someone else, but I can still hear her. "It's some guy who says he's that Jennifer girl's boyfriend."

The person she's talking to says something back, but I can't really hear it. I think she said "awkward." Why would she say that?

The girl, whoever she is, doesn't pick the phone up again. I can't hear what's going on except some faint voices in the background and some music playing. I don't recognize the music.

That whole world, that whole theater world, is just so bizarre to me. I don't get it.

Someone picks up the phone. "Hello?" It's Jennifer.

"Jenn, oh my God, I'm so happy to hear your voice. You're not going to believe what happened tonight." I start laughing because I'm just so happy to have finally gotten her on the phone.

"Luke? Is that you?"

"Yeah. It's me. I'm so sorry. I tried to call. You won't believe how hard it was to try and call you. I couldn't get the party line to work because of this asshole who lives here. And then I tried to get cell reception and then I got chased by a fucking dog. And then I actually broke into someone's house. Okay, can you believe that? I actually like practically committed a felony to try and talk to you."

"Luke?"

"Yeah, Jennifer. It's me."

"I can barely hear you."

"You can't? Oh shit. This isn't a cell phone. You should be able to hear me."

"Luke, can you hear me? I can't really hear you. Listen, if you can hear me, a bunch of us are sitting around in my room watching *Casablanca*. Okay? So I'm really sad I didn't get to talk to you tonight, but I miss you, okay?"

"What, you're hanging up?"

"Yeah, I gotta go."

"So we're not going to even talk?"

"No, I can't hear you. I'm sorry. Okay, bye."

She hung up the phone. She hung up the fucking phone. I can't fucking believe that. What is that about? I mean, with what I went through tonight. I've been trying all night just to talk to her, but I don't even get to say anything to her?

What is that? It's not fair. That's not fair. Come on, this can't be happening to me.

Wait, what just happened? If she couldn't hear me, then why could the other girl? And plus, she seemed like she could hear me at the end there. That seemed fine.

At the end I was like, "You can't hear me?" And she was like, "No, I've got to go." That was fucking bullshit. She was lying to me.

I can't believe she was lying to me.

Oh God, fucking A. This is total bullshit. Fuck it. I'm just going to—I don't know.

I can't even think. Fuck me, this can't really be happening.

The breeze picks up outside and a wind chime sounds.

This is stupid. I hang up the phone. Fuck, I just realized where I'm standing. What if the minister comes home and sees me in his house? I've got to get out of here. I go out the same way I came, but a lot faster. I close the sliding glass door behind me and I try to remember if anything else was different from when I came in. It's dark and their wind chimes are making a lot of noise. I wonder where the minister is.

I run off his property to our property. I stop next to the dying crab apple tree. I can see right into our windows because Mom and Dad never close the drapes. They're in there talking.

I'm standing here, looking in the windows of my own house, and I don't want to go back in there. I could very easily just walk in and go into my room, but I know they'd try and talk to me and ask me where I've been, and I don't want to talk about it.

I just realized I'm standing right in the sweet spot of the neighborhood. I'm about twenty-five feet from my cottage, and the same distance from all the other cottages. No-man's-land.

The crickets are chirping in the darkness, looking for a date, I guess. And the bullfrogs are doing the same. I used to like how quiet the cottage was in the summer. No other people, no cars, no horns. No nothing. But now, as I look at it, it just feels empty.

I turn around and look at the minister's cottage behind me, and then the Richardsons' and their stone wall, then ours, then the Vizquels'. I keep turning so that I feel a little dizzy. I like this feeling. I used to love to spin around in circles when I was a little kid. I spin faster, so the lights from the cottages look like they're all connected. This is like a carnival ride. This is fun, except I'm completely miserable. I've got nowhere to go. I've got nowhere to be. I let myself fall on the grass and lie on my back looking up at the trees. I'll just lie here until everyone else goes to bed. I can't face talking to anyone else tonight.

I'm going to go inside and go to bed. Mom and Dad are in bed finally. It took them forever. I hold the screen door so it doesn't slam and then tiptoe down the hall past Mom and Dad's room.

"Good night, honey," says Mom from her bed. I go into my room and get in bed. I don't even brush my teeth. I just get in bed.

All those nights we spent together. For what?

Maybe I'll write a poem about this. Or a song.

> There's nothing left for me to do.
>> Nothing left, 'cause, baby,
>> I love you.
> Something inside of me is gone.
>> I cannot make it all alone.
> I tried so hard to make it right.
>> You're probably doing it with Mike.
> I wanted you so very much.
>> You wanted to play double Dutch.

Well, that was pretty good, right up until the line about double Dutch. Whatever, it doesn't matter. I wasn't really going to write anything about this anyway.

I'm still awake. Something feels wrong. The whole world feels dirtier and grimier than it did before. Why am I still sleeping in a bed with *Star Wars* sheets? Why do I have an *E.T.* poster on my wall?

The lake is about the only thing that will make me feel better. My bathing suit is hanging on the line out back of the cottage. I grab it and change right in the middle of the living room. Nobody is up anyway. It doesn't matter.

The grass is wet and spongy, and my feet feel like they're sinking as I walk across our yard.

I look at the minister's cottage as I pass by. His van still isn't there. I hope that little girl isn't in there all alone. That would be really creepy. Maybe I should tell Mom about it and she could call social services.

Damn it, I hate it here. The only things I can think about are the Richardsons and the minister and the fucking property lines. The wall. Jennifer. How much I miss her. I remember when I could go weeks without worrying about anything; now I've got so much trouble on my mind. It sucks.

The night is cool, and I feel like it's early September even though it's still July. I walk down to the water, over the same old stones I've walked on millions of times, and take off my shirt. I step into the lake and walk in up to my knees. The water actually feels warm for once, probably because it's so cool tonight. I take a deep breath and go in up to my waist. That's always the hardest part.

I keep going up to my chest and then slip underwater, so slowly that the surface tension makes the water feel like mercury. My whole head goes under and I swim underwater in the night through the green light. There's nothing to see, but I keep my eyes wide open. I swim all the way down to the bottom of the lake and run my hands over the stones and sand and mud.

I twist around and kick my feet and swim so hard and so fast that I feel like a dolphin. A freshwater dolphin.

I'm running out of breath, so I bring myself back up to the surface and come up so that only my eyes come out of the water at first, then my nose so I can get a breath of air again.

At least this is peaceful. At least all my troubles don't follow me out here into the middle of the lake. I tilt my head back and look up at the stars. There are a billion of them. If there are billions of stars, then maybe the other stuff that happens in life doesn't really matter too much.

I remember when I was little and I used to think everything was so boring. Or I'd worry and worry and worry about stupid stuff and get all caught up in it. When I was little, I used to wish I were older, just so I could grow up, but now I don't wish anything. Actually, I'm going to try something different.

I'm just going to wish that I'm here and I'm living right now. Maybe that sounds obvious, but I'm going to try that. I'm going to try and live life like it's happening to me right now, right at the moment. I'm going to let everything come to me. Whatever happens, that's going to be it. I'm just going to try and appreciate life.

I close my eyes and tip my head back so my ears go underwater. Silence. That's the key. Silence is the key to life.

I bring my head back up. Wait, that's stupid. Silence isn't the key to life. I hate silence. The whole point of life is that it's not silent. I don't want to be some Buddhist monk living alone on a fucking mountaintop.

Damn it, this isn't working. I swim back toward shore, back to where my life and all my problems are.

Roger, Kay, and Claire showed up after breakfast. We're all going to a baseball game later, and they're spending the day here. This is the last thing I need. I just want it to be like *I*

Am Legend and have it just be me and Jennifer. Us, the only people on earth. We could repopulate the planet. That would be fun.

I don't think that Claire has ever had a boyfriend. I guess I'll force myself to go and make fun of her about that. At least that'll help pass the time until I get to talk to Jennifer and straighten things out.

Claire is sitting at the kitchen table playing solitaire. Perfect, I don't know why she even comes out here if she hates being outside so much.

I sit down across from her and look at the cards. I'm not really in the mood to do this, but I will anyway. I say, "Hi, Claire."

"Hello, Luke." She says that like she's not that happy to see me. I don't know why she wouldn't be.

"How's it going?"

"*Great.*" She sounds so sarcastic it's ridiculous.

"You're not having fun?"

"No, I'm having a *great* time."

"Sure. Sure. Of course you are." I pause. How am I going to get into making fun of her? Got it. "So, I just talked to my girlfriend."

"Good for you."

"Yes, it was good for me. It was very good. Do you have a boyfriend?"

"I have lots of friends."

"Any of them boys?"

"Some of them are boys." Defensive, I like it.

"Are any of them boyfriends?"

"Yes, I have boy friends."

"But do you have a boyfriend?" She doesn't say anything. I've got her. I keep going. "You know, a boyfriend, like a serious boyfriend who you do stuff with and fool around with and stuff. A boyfriend."

"I don't have time for that."

I got her to admit that she doesn't have a boyfriend. "Don't have time for that? Don't have time for that? No time for romance? For sweet stolen kisses and chocolates and long strolls on the beach?"

"No." I can tell she's getting angry.

"Well, do you have a girlfriend?"

"No." Angrier.

"Any friends who are girls who you sometimes have sleepovers with? Have little experimental make-out sessions with? Practicing?"

"No." She is white-hot, but she's not boiling over. What can I do to make her boil over? Hmm. "Have you ever been kissed? You know, a little spin the bottle. Downstairs in the basement. Parents upstairs. Boy with his tongue down your throat and his hand up your shirt."

No response. This is very good. One more little thing and I'll get her to blow. What should it be? Sex? She's obviously never had sex. That's too easy.

I make my voice nice and quiet, like I'm her friend or her mother. "You know, Claire, some people just take a little longer to develop personal relationships. That doesn't mean that you're never going to have a boyfriend. And it doesn't mean that you're never going to get married or have kids. Claire, just remember—"

"Shut up! Shut the fuck up! Okay, I've never had a boyfriend. Okay, are you happy? I've never made out with a scummy creep in the basement, okay? I don't want to do that. Especially if the boy is going to act anything at all like you."

She stands up and blows past me out the door. I watch her go all the way down to the water. Oh great, she's going to go and tell our parents that I made fun of her, just like always, and then they're going to come and yell at me.

But she doesn't even talk to them. She just lies down on a beach towel and puts another one over her face.

Now I feel like an asshole. What a pain in my balls. I'm going back to bed.

Mom comes into my room. I wish she would learn how to knock. She's holding a postcard. Oh wow, it must be from Jennifer. I need to call her.

It's a postcard of the movie poster for *Casablanca*. That's right, didn't she watch that movie the other night with a bunch of people? I think she did.

I take the postcard from Mom and turn it over. It's one of Jennifer's haiku. I read it and read it again. Wait, I don't get it. Is this a joke? Is there another postcard that came along with this one?

I look up at Mom and I'm about to ask her, but she mouths the word "sorry."

I read it again just to make sure that it says what I think it says.

> Casablanca *is*
> *the world's most romantic film.*
> *I slept with someone.*

Hold on, this can't be right. This is all wrong. Where's the phone? I've got to call her. I go out to the living room and grab the phone. I dial the number from the other night.

"Hello?" some girl says.

"Jennifer?" I know it's not her.

"No. Who's calling?"

"Uh, it doesn't matter. Is she there?"

"Hold on." She puts down the phone and screams, "Jennifer!" She pauses and then says, "She's not here."

"Well, do you have any idea where she is?"

"No."

"Does anyone?"

"I don't know."

"Well, can you ask?"

She puts her hand over the phone and calls out to whoever is there, "Does anyone know where Jennifer is?"

I can't hear if anyone is responding. I just want to hear it. I just want to hear someone say something. I look out the window. Claire is standing in the yard talking to the minister's little girl. Why is she doing that?

The girl gets back on the phone. "Someone says she might be at the costume shop."

"Really? What's that? Do you have that number?"

"Hold on." She yells again, "Do they have a phone there?"

There's a pause. I feel like I'm in space without a helmet. She comes back on. "Here it is. You ready?"

"Yeah." I write down the number and call it as soon as the girl gets off the phone. It rings for a thousand years.

"Costume shop."

"Hi, is someone named Jennifer there?"

"This is Jennifer." Oh my God, I didn't recognize her voice.

"Jenn. It's me."

"Oh, hi." She's whispering. She doesn't want anyone to know she's on the phone.

"I got your postcard. Is that a joke what you wrote?"

"Which one? The cow one?"

"No. The *Casablanca* one."

"Oh, that one. You got that already? I just sent it like yesterday. That's amazing. Can you believe they'll carry a postcard all the way to New York for twenty-six cents? I wouldn't take a postcard to the next room for twenty-six cents."

I don't even know if she's talking to me. I say, "Are you talking to me?"

"Of course I am."

"It just sounds like you're talking to someone else."

"Who?"

"I don't know. Someone you don't know."

"I know you."

"I know."

"Do you?"

"What?" Am I going crazy?

"Do you know that I know you?"

"I guess."

"Then you know me too, right? You know me too."

"What do you mean?"

"You know me too."

"Yeah, I guess." I am going crazy.

"So you know that I wrote that, and you know what it means."

"Um, wait. What are we talking about? What are you saying?"

"I'm just saying that you know me. So you know how hard it was for me to write that. You know how hard it is for me to open up."

"No. Wait. I'm lost."

"I wrote that because it's true. I just wanted to be honest with you."

"You wanted to be honest."

"Yeah, so that's why I wrote that. I'm trying to be honest with you."

"Hold on. So you wrote that poem, that fucking haiku, to be honest with me? To be honest?"

"Don't swear at me."

"I'm not. I'm just swearing at the situation. You slept with someone. You're saying you fucking slept with someone?"

"Yes, I was just being honest."

"And this is how I find out? You tell me?" That's a line from a Steve Martin movie. I don't know why I said that. I guess I wanted her to laugh or something, because she loves that movie. She doesn't laugh, though.

I say, "So, can you tell me what happened?"

"It's just like I wrote on the postcard."

"So there's nothing else to say?"

"No. Not really. Do you really want to know?"

"Um, yeah. I want to know. Tell me." I don't know if I want to know, but I also don't want to stop talking to her. I want her to apologize or something, or at least feel a little bit bad.

"I met someone. A guy."

"What's his name?"

"Nathan."

"Jesus, Nathan? The guy's name is Nathan?" I can hear Mom in the other room doing something. I hope she's not listening to this.

"Yes. Do you want to know more?"

"Yes, tell me more."

"Do you really?"

"Yeah. Tell me." I don't, but I can't stop myself.

"We watched *Casablanca*."

"Uh-huh."

"And it was incredibly romantic."

"Uh-huh."

"And then we slept together."

I don't say anything.

"Do you want to know more?"

I can't really think. It's like she just poured boiling water into my ear. Do I want to know more? No, I don't. "Is that the only time? Is that the only time you slept together?"

"No. We also watched *Dawn of the Dead* and then slept together again."

"Really? A zombie movie? That's what puts you in the mood? That's fucked up."

"You don't have to insult me."

"I do, actually. I actually do have to insult you. That's one of the things a boyfriend has to do when his girlfriend sleeps with someone else. He has to insult her, so get used to it." Mom drops something in the next room.

"Why are you being mean?"

"Uh, hmmm, why am I being mean? I don't know, I guess I don't have a reason to be mean, other than you slept with another guy—twice."

"Yeah, are you mad?" Her voice softens a little.

"No, I'm not mad." Did I just say I'm not mad? I am mad. "Wait, no, I am mad. I'm actually very mad at you. You shouldn't have done that. Why did you do that?"

"I don't know. We're only sixteen—it's not like we were going to get married."

That's funny. I sort of thought we were going to get married. I guess we don't have anything else to say to each other. "Okay, I'm going to hang up on you now." I hang up the phone. I slam down the receiver so hard that the bell inside it rings. I almost pick it up to see if it's Jennifer calling back, but I catch myself. I think I might have broken the phone. I go back to my room.

I'm a mummy. I'm King Tut. All my organs have been cut out and replaced with sawdust. My skin has been wrapped in papyrus and my eyes have been removed.

Mom opens the door and asks if I want to go to the baseball game with Roger, Kay, and Claire, but I can't speak. I'm a sarcophagus.

It's ten-fourteen. I've been lying in here for I don't know how long. What am I supposed to do? This is so stupid. So fucking stupid. I can't go to sleep, because I'm not even tired. I try and relax and close my eyes. I take a deep breath to try and pull in all of that creek summer smell, but it doesn't smell the same tonight. It smells like someone is burning something somewhere. Like a pile of leaves or something. But I've smelled burning leaves before, and this doesn't smell like burning leaves. This smells like a bonfire, or not even like a bonfire. This smells like a fire. Is something on fire?

I get up out of bed and walk down the hall. The smell is even stronger out here. I go into the kitchen and check the stove, but it's not on. There's no candles or anything. There's nothing. But there's still the smell. The wind picks up and I can hear the branches of the walnut tree scraping the roof.

Where is that smell coming from? I wonder if there was lightning that hit a tree, but I didn't hear any thunder. I go over to the window and look up at the trees. There's nothing. I can't see anything, anyway.

All I can see is the minister's house. He's got all his lights on but his van isn't in the driveway. Wait. Is that fire? Is his house on fire? Oh shit, his house is on fire. Fuck. Fucking shit.

"Mom! Dad!"

I don't hear anything in the back bedroom. This is bad. This isn't happening fast enough. "There's a fire! There's a fire at the minister's house!"

No one is coming. I forgot they went out to a baseball game and then dinner. They're not back yet.

What should I do? Call 911.

I pick up the phone, but there's no dial tone. Fuck, I think I did break it. It doesn't work. What should I do? Go wake the Richardsons.

I open the screen door, run across the lawn, jump over the wall, and knock on their door. Shit, everything is taking too long. I can hear the fire now. It's crackling.

"Mr. Richardson! Fire! Call 911!"

A light goes on in the bedroom on the first floor, and I run over to the open window. Mr. Richardson says, "What's happening out there?"

"Fire, Mr. Richardson. Call 911."

There's a pause and then he says, "I can't find my glasses. Come on in and call."

I run back around to the front door and let myself in. There's a phone on the wall. I dial the numbers 9-1-1.

"Nine-one-one, what is your emergency?"

"Fire. A fire in a cottage near the lake."

"What is your location?"

"Uh, the lake road, about halfway down . . ."

Mr. Richardson walks into the kitchen. I guess he found his glasses. He takes the phone from me and gives them the exact address.

He listens on the phone for a second and says, "No, there's no one in the house."

Oh shit, I just remembered. There might be a little girl. "There might be a little girl."

"What?" Mr. Richardson stares at me. "A girl? He says there's a little girl."

I'm out the door and running across the lawn. The fire is inside the house. The whole thing looks like a lantern. That little girl is in there. Oh God.

Why isn't anyone doing anything? Mr. Richardson has come out with his garden hose and he's trying to spray the house from halfway across his lawn. Mrs. Richardson is out in her nightgown, just standing there watching like it's a bonfire.

At least the house has stone on the outside—otherwise I think it would be gone already. The fire's getting bigger inside, though. It's got most of the drapes. It's going to get the ceiling, and then the roof is going to go. They've got to hurry.

"Mr. Richardson. How long did they say?"

"Twenty minutes."

"Twenty minutes? Mr. Richardson, the whole house is going to be gone by then."

He looks at me like I'm an idiot. "What do you want me to do about it?"

I don't know. I don't know what I want anyone to do about it. But what if the little girl is home? We can't just sit here and watch it burn. We've got to do something. Anything. Can't anyone do anything?

I know where she'd be. I watched her go into that bedroom the other day. Come on. Come on. I can get to her. I can save her.

"I've got to go in there," I say to no one.

"No," Mr. Richardson says.

"There's a kid in there. A girl. I know where she is."

"I'll go."

"I know where she is, though. I can do it."

"No. I'm not letting you go in there. It's not safe. Your parents—"

"But we've got to hurry. The fire's burning. It's a kid."

"Let it burn."

He stares at me. I can't tell what he's thinking. But I don't care. I'm going in there.

I've got it pictured in my head. I know how to do it. I know what to do. "Mrs. Richardson, get a bunch of blankets. Heavy blankets. We'll soak the blankets with the hose."

They're hesitating. We can't hesitate. We've got to move. I scream at them, "Go!" Now they're moving. Mr. Richardson heads back to his house. Where is he going? "Mrs. Richardson, buckets?"

Mrs. Richardson nods her head and runs over to their garage.

I can't wait any longer. I've got to go for a swim. I run down to the beach, just like I used to when I was a kid. My feet are tough enough to handle the rocks, and I sprint until I'm knee-deep in the water, and then I dive all the way in.

I'm out before I even get in, but I get my hair wet enough to keep the fire off me, I hope.

I run back up the beach, across the lawn, and to the minister's house. Mr. Richardson comes up behind me and puts a long, heavy wool coat on me. He's already soaked it. It must weigh a hundred pounds. He holds his big rain boots for me to put on. They're filled with water too. I slip my feet into the boots, and Mrs. Richardson piles wet blankets over my head.

I'm about to open the sliding glass door when Mr. Richardson calls me back. "Cool Hand Luke," he says. He holds up a pair of leather work gloves.

That's a good idea. I forgot about my hands. I put them on and dunk them in Mrs. Richardson's bucket of water and go back to the glass door. I can't really see with these blankets over my head. I can just barely make out the shape of the sliding glass door. I pull it open and the heat comes at me all at once.

The air is so hot I can't even breathe it. It's like that sauna air, but four or five times hotter. I step back and take a few breaths of the air I can breathe.

Whatever water was on me has evaporated. I step into the house and start walking toward the girl's bedroom. The fire is loud all around me, like the crowd at a baseball game.

I hear wood cracking somewhere. I hope it doesn't fall on me. I didn't realize I was holding my breath. I can't tell where I'm going. My eyes keep closing. The fire is too hot even for my eyes.

I let out a little air and try and suck it back in, but all the smoke. I forgot there would be smoke. Come on, where is that door? Stupid door.

I cough out all the smoke, but there's nothing left to breathe now. It's okay to hold your breath when there's some air in your lungs, but I'm trying to hold it with them empty, so nothing can get in. Oh God. Oh fuck. This was really stupid.

Shit. I shouldn't have come in here. I'm going to die in

here. I turn around and start looking for the exit signs. There's supposed to be exit signs. I go down to my knees.

There's more air down here. I can almost breathe it. The door. The girl. Door. Handle. Turn. Open. Close.

I'm in. I'm in. There's no fire in here. Thank God. I can breathe more. But there's no girl either. There's no girl. I look in the bed. No girl. Where's the girl? She was supposed to be here. She wasn't just a dream or something, right? She should be here. What if she's not here?

Come on, girl. Where are you? Where the hell would you be? I didn't come in here just to die. Where are you? Under the bed? No. Under the covers? No. I take the blankets off my head so I can see better. Maybe she wasn't in this bedroom. Maybe she was in the one next door.

I don't know if I can get out of here. The fire is so hot out there. I'm sweating, but it's so hot it's just evaporating right off my skin. If I could just find her, I'd be able to open that window and then jump right out. I don't know, I might have to do that anyway.

I'm giving up. This was stupid.

I go over to the window. There's no latch. There's no knob or anything. Does this window open? I push on it and pull on it. It's like a wall. Nothing is moving. Oh fuck me. I'm going to die in here.

Fuck. Come on. This is such a stupid way to die. I don't want to die like this. I'm panicking. Don't panic. I turn around and look back at the room.

The closet. I didn't check there, did I? Is she in there? Is she?

That's her. There she is. Curled up on the floor. Oh my God.

"I'm going to get you out of here, okay?"

She's not saying anything, but she's looking right at me.

I scoop her up and carry her over to the window. I need something to break it with. Something hard. There are dolls everywhere and stuffed animals. Shit. No dinosaurs. No rock collection. Wait, there's a perfect rock right on her bedside table. It's a skipping rock. She's got a skipping rock on her bedside table.

I pick it up and sidearm it as hard as I can right through the window. It smashes, but there are all sorts of jagged pieces of glass. Too sharp to climb over. I punch them out with my leather gloves and lay a blanket over the glass to make it safe enough for the little girl.

I pick her up and push her through the window feetfirst and then she drops to the ground. It's only a few feet. I climb through headfirst. Dad's here. Oh my God, Dad's here. He pulls me out the rest of the way, pulls me away from the house, and lays me down on the soft pine needles. Mom has the girl. Finally, I can breathe.

Thank God, I can breathe.

I'm inside an ambulance, going fast, looking up at two big lights and a woman in a ponytail. I'm okay. I don't like this plastic mask on my face. It smells too much like plastic. I try and take it off, but the woman yells at me to leave it on. The girl is next to me. They're paying more attention to her. That's good. I hope she's okay. They're going to take good care of her, I hope. I hope she's okay.

I'm okay. I don't hurt anywhere, except my knees and it's hard to get a good breath. I say, "Is she okay?" but nobody hears me. It's too loud with the sirens and them all talking.

I wonder if she's dying. I hope she's not dying. I turn my head and look at her. She's looking at me. She blinks and keeps looking at me. She's got an oxygen mask on, like me.

I want to reach out and hold her hand and tell her that she's going to be okay. "Hey, you're going to be okay. Okay?" I say, but I don't think she can hear me.

The people working on her are trying to get her attention, but she just keeps looking at me. I reach out my hand.

She reaches her hand out too, but we can't quite touch. The IV in my arm is tugging a little and her arms are really short. I point my index finger out at her, and she points hers at me.

The woman in the ponytail pulls the little girl's arm back in. Shit, what's her name? I don't even know her name.

I pull off my oxygen mask and say, "What's her name?" My voice sounds like it belongs to an old alcoholic comedian who smoked cigars his whole life.

"What's her name?" I say it louder.

The ponytail lady hears me and looks over her shoulder. The girl is saying something and the ponytail lady leans down to hear it.

"Amelie. Her name is Amelie." She says it so matter-of-factly, like it's not the prettiest name in the world.

I'll go to the hospital for a while. I just want to make sure that Amelie is going to be okay and then I'll go home.

They say they want to keep me overnight for observation. That's what they say, but I think it's bullshit. They say I inhaled so much smoke when I was in there that they want to make sure my lungs are working right. It does feel like I had a barbecue inside my chest. I keep coughing and I can't stop, like everything in there is a little char-grilled.

My parents say Amelie is okay. She's in another part of the hospital, but she's going to be okay.

I want to call Jennifer. I want to tell her about what happened, and maybe when she hears, she'll dump that guy and she'll come up here and spend the rest of the summer with me.

I tell Mom that I need to call Jennifer, and she works it out with the nurses how to make a long-distance call from the room. She has to dial a bunch of numbers to make it work with her credit card. She hands me the phone and leaves the room.

I don't know if I remember the phone number. Fuck, what was it? It's in my head, but I'm just too tired to get it out.

I'll try and call tomorrow. I hang up and close my eyes.

Kay, Roger, and Claire are in the hospital to visit. Kay and Roger are sitting by the hospital bed and Claire is standing in the back of the room. She hasn't made eye contact with me yet.

Mom is saying something to Kay about how the fire might have started. It sounds like the police are investigating it.

I don't care about that. It doesn't matter. Everyone's fine. It doesn't matter.

Claire is still standing at the back of the room. I want to tell her I'm sorry, but I don't know exactly the right way to put it. Fuck, when was the last time I had to apologize to Claire? When I hit her in the head with that chestnut when we were six.

Dad asks Roger if they will bring over dinner and stay the night after I get out of the hospital. Roger says sure, they'll be happy to help out. Dad says, "Don't forget the peppermint stick ice cream."

Good, maybe I can apologize to her later.

They release me from the hospital after one night and we all drive home together like a family, down the same highways we drive when we're arriving for the first time. Mom tells me that Amelie is doing okay but they're keeping her in for observation for another day.

Dad is telling me they wrote about it in the paper and a reporter from the newspaper wants to interview me. They want to take my picture and talk to me about what happened. I can't help but think that it doesn't even matter. Nothing seems like it matters anymore.

I just want to talk to Jennifer. I miss her. She doesn't even know what happened. She doesn't even know. I want to tell her the whole story. It won't even seem real until she knows about it.

We drive down the old lake road, past the Wirth mansion and the house that looks like a tepee. I remember when I was a little kid and this drive was like the most exciting thing that ever happened to me. I remember it was just the best thing ever. I wish I could get back to that.

I wish that it were somehow possible to go back and relive it all again, but without wanting to grow up so fast. Just to take it slow and be cool and enjoy being a little kid and running through the wet grass with bare feet. The feel of the stones when we first get here. How I'd try and run across the stones until my feet got tough enough so I didn't feel it anymore.

I wish I could still do that. I wish I could carry myself like that, like nothing mattered but the sunlight and the time of day.

We drive down the road, past the Vizquels', and there's the minister's cottage. All the windows are gone, and so is most of the roof, but the rest of the house is still standing. There's broken glass everywhere.

I feel sick to my stomach just looking at it. I hope that it's not always going to look like that.

There's a basket of fresh strawberries on the front step of the cottage. I look around and I see Sophie sitting at a picnic table in her front yard. She's reading a book and looking up at me every few seconds.

I want to call out to her, but I don't. I don't because I feel stupid. I've never talked to her before. We've never wanted to be friends with the Vizquels. I don't know why we're like that.

I raise my hand to wave to her, and Sophie looks up from her book and waves back to me. Both my parents look surprised that I just did that. I smile at her, and she smiles at me and then goes back to reading her book.

That was so easy. I've got this smile on my face that I can't get rid of. It's just a little thing, but it feels so good. I could go over and talk to her, but I don't. I could, though. At least now I could go over there and say hi if I wanted to.

I go into the bedroom, lie down on the bottom bunk, and close my eyes.

I look at the clock. It's ten-thirty-seven. I can't believe I slept all day. But I can't sleep anymore. I'm too hot. I have to get out of here. I can't breathe in here, it's so hot tonight. My lungs feel hot. I open my door, go down the hall, and see Roger and Kay asleep on the pullout couch. Shit, I forgot they were here.

I go back to my room, unhook the eyehole latch on my window, and push out the screen into the grass below. That was a little loud. I stop for a second and listen for my mom's voice, but I don't hear anything. I sit on the sill, swing my legs out into the night air, and step down onto the spongy grass outside the window.

The Richardsons' house is totally dark and there's no car in the driveway. I turn left at the old pine tree and walk past the woodpile and the new stone wall. The moon is out and the trees cast long blue shadows across the Richardsons' lawn and onto what's left of the minister's house. I can smell the burned mattresses and carpet from here.

I walk up to the edge of the caution tape and try to look in. Only the outside walls are left. There's nothing but black on the inside. I know I was in there, but I can't really remember the feeling of being in there, of being in the middle of all that fire. The only thing I remember is Amelie in her tiny pink nightgown and how when I picked her up, she felt as light as a blanket. She could have died in there. I feel sick. I need to go for a swim. I turn around and see the Richardsons' house. Mr. Richardson's bedroom window faces the minister's house. How could he not have known that the house was on fire? Why the fuck did it take him so long to get his glasses and talk to the 911 operator?

I look back at the minister's house. Why did he leave that little girl home alone all the time? Where was he? Why did it have to fucking turn out like this?

Nothing will ever be the same. I walk away from the houses and head down to the water.

Oh shit, there's a person sitting on the rocks over at the edge of the lake. Who is that? Mr. Richardson? It couldn't be.

No, it's a girl. It's Claire. She's looking out at the lake. I walk closer and come around from the side. She's wearing a sweatshirt with the hood pulled way over so I can't see her face. Her knees are pulled up inside and they're sticking out the neck. She's tapping her toes in the water.

I walk over. "Hey, Claire."

She looks up at me and says, in a voice so quiet I can barely hear her, "Hi, Luke. I'm glad you're okay."

"Me too."

She opens her mouth like she's about to say something else, but she stops and looks away. I sit down on the rocks about six feet away from her. I understand why she doesn't want to look at me. It's because I gave her shit for being a virgin and because of all the rest of the crap I pulled over the years. I feel bad about all the times I tortured her. I don't know what my problem was. I wish I could start over with her.

We stare out at the water, without saying anything, for ten thousand years.

I can't stand it any longer. "Claire?" My voice fills up the night. She doesn't answer.

"Hey, I'm sorry." She doesn't say anything back. "I'm really sorry about the way I treated you. It wasn't fair and it wasn't right, and it's not an excuse, but my girlfriend was in the process of dumping me, and I think I sort of went a little crazy. So, I'm sorry and I really hope that you can forgive me, because I didn't mean to be such an asshole. And I know I was one." I stop and look over at her. She's got her head down on her knees. "So, anyway, yeah, I'm sorry."

The night takes up the silence. I hear a plane engine far away and I look up at the sky. There's a flashing red dot traveling across the stars. I wonder if that's a plane, or a UFO, or maybe a satellite.

I look back at Claire. She hasn't moved. Okay. Here goes. "I also want to apologize for all the other times I messed with you when you were playing solitaire. And also for all the times I called you a mini-parent." I'm not getting any response, so I go on. "Claire, I'm also sorry that I hit you in the head with that chestnut when we were six. And I know I was mean to you when we were playing on the same T-ball team, and I'm sorry about that too." She's still not looking at me, but I think she's starting to smile.

"I'm also sorry that I said 'Shut up' in your yard that time. And for the flood in my room that you got partially blamed for. Also, I'd like to say I'm sorry for the time that I told you to lie down in the road and then tried to jump my bike over you. And I'm sorry that I punched you after you told on me for killing the minnows." She's really trying not to laugh. I keep going.

"I'm also sorry about making fun of how your dog had one eye that was blue and one eye that was brown. That was actually a really cool thing about that dog, and I think I was just jealous." She laughs out loud. "And I'm sorry that I made fun of the way your mom makes peanut butter and jelly sandwiches."

She stops laughing, holds up her hand like she wants me to stop, and says, "Wait, you made fun of the way my mom makes peanut butter and jelly?"

"Yeah, I don't like the way she puts butter on the bread before the peanut butter."

"Really? I love that. It's so good."

Now we're both laughing in the dark and looking out at the lake and the billion stars reflecting off the black water. I glance over at her. "So, what do you think? Can you forgive me?"

"Yeah, I think I can manage a little bit of forgiveness."

"Really? For everything?"

"Not for everything. I'm still mad about that chestnut. My mom had to cut it out of my hair."

"Sorry about that."

"And also, you used to make fun of my retainer. That was really shitty."

I laugh because it's funny to hear her swear. "Oh yeah, I called you Coin, because you looked like you were sucking on a coin. I forgot about that. I'm a jerk. I'm sorry."

"It's okay. Apology accepted. Really and truly."

"Thank you. Really and truly." We look at each other for just a second, and I feel good for the first time on this trip.

I lean over and pick up a perfect skipping stone sitting right there in front of me. I stand up and fling it nice and easy and it skips like a whisper across the water. The moon is so bright I can see every time it hits the water.

She says, "Oh, I have something for you." She reaches into her pocket, pulls out something small, and holds it up. I reach down and take it out of her hand. I can tell right away what it is. It's a luckystone about as big as a quarter. "I found it when you were in the hospital. I figured it was meant for you."

I close my hand around it. "Thank you, Claire. I've been looking for one of these for a long time."

The wind pushes the upper limbs above us, and a dog yelps across the creek and pulls against its chain.

I say, "Hey, do you want to do something?"

"What, like something bad?"

I laugh. "No. Do you want to take the canoe out?"

"Now?"

"Yeah, now. Come on, there's enough light to see by."

She looks up at the night sky, then back at the cottage. "But if my parents wake up and I'm not here, they'll be worried."

"We'll be back way before they wake up."

"Then yes."

"Yes?"

"I said yes."

I put the luckystone in my pocket and offer her my hand. She takes it and I pull her up to her feet. We go up the beach and each grab an end of the canoe, flip it over, and drag it down the rocks into the water. The wood rubs and scrapes against all the stones. It's really loud. It's a good thing the Richardsons aren't here.

She gets in the front and gets the paddle out. I push off the stones and hop into the back, and we glide out into the silent water. Her blond hair takes the color of the moonlight, and she pushes up the sleeves of her sweatshirt like she's about to do some really serious work. She's got such skinny wrists. I never noticed that before. I could touch my thumb and my pinkie around those wrists.

She paddles on the left side. I paddle on the right and we head straight out, toward the twinkling lights on the other side of the lake. I watch her paddle push the water into little whirlpool spirals, like bathwater draining. We keep going and going until we get all the way out into the middle of the lake, until it's just us in our boat surrounded by water.

We stop and rest the paddles on our knees and drift. We're both out of breath. I look way down the lake at the smokestacks, like two fingers pointing toward heaven, and up the lake to the places I've never been to. I realize I don't even know what's up there. I turn the bow so that I can see our little cove.

I don't know if it's the night or the moon or how far away we are, but our cottage and the other cottages all the way up and down the lake, they all look pretty much the same. The only thing that makes me sure which cove is ours is the Confederate flag at the end of the minister's dock. The breeze picks up for a moment and the flag catches it like a sail, but the water stays still.

Claire puts her paddle back in the water. I put mine in too and we paddle slowly back toward shore, watching the cottages getting farther apart the closer we get.

I look back over my shoulder. The lake has turned into black glass with silver ribbons where the moonlight catches the ripples we leave behind.

Nothing stays the same. And maybe that's okay. Maybe that's the way it should be.

ACKNOWLEDGMENTS

Christina Egloff was my collaborator on this book from first page to last. She has the rarest talent—to take whatever she touches and spin it into something better. She's an artist Rumpelstiltskin.